BETWEEN WORLDS 3

THE FIRST STEP

LORI WOLF-HEFFNER

HEAD IN THE GROUND PUBLISHING

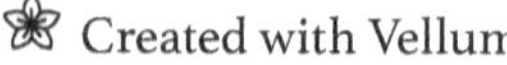 Created with Vellum

Dedicated to Peter Tork (1942-2019), who's now stomping his hands and clapping his feet with Davy.

CHAPTER ONE

Juliana shook her head as she looked out the window. All that snow from two weeks ago had melted and the dead appearance of winter showed itself everywhere. She checked the weather on her phone: six degrees Celsius.

"I don't know how people here can live like this," she said to herself. "What on earth am I supposed to wear today?"

She looked at the time on her phone, wishing she could call Rachel. But Rachel, back in Calgary, would be asleep.

Juliana turned on some music to lift her mood and to get rid of some of her nervousness: today was her first day of high school in Kitchener. She began shaking out her limbs, the old bungalow's floor creaking beneath her. As the music's energy built up inside her, Juliana danced around her tiny room, calming herself down.

But she couldn't dance in her pyjamas all day. Quickly, she pulled on a pair of jean leggings and a loose, bulky, cream-coloured sweater that reached mid-thigh. She slid in dangling earrings and hung a Fairtrade necklace with large, colourful beads on her neck.

Now for her hair. But would it hold in this weather? Or should she just tie it up? She did a quick French twist across the front and tucked the tail of the twist behind her ear.

"No, that's too formal."

Juliana wrapped her hair into a bun and held it in place with her hand. "No. I already have to wear this for ballet."

She could search for ideas online, but another look at her phone told her she wouldn't have time to learn a new style.

"Maybe I should braid it." Juliana glanced over at the old leather notebook that lay on her night table. It was a collection of drawings Omama—her great-grandmother—had made almost one hundred years before. In those days, women covered their hair with a *haube*—a white bonnet that fit close to the head—or a headscarf or both. Girls usually wore their hair uncovered but always braided. "Nope. I don't want to look like I'm a hundred years old either."

She glanced at her phone again. "Rachel, can't you wake up early?"

"Juliana!" Mom called from the kitchen. "Breakfast!"

Only now did Juliana notice her favourite breakfast smell: bacon, hash browns, and eggs.

"Coming!" Juliana turned off her phone, studied her look in the mirror, and whipped her hair up into a ponytail. She could worry about a better hairstyle tomorrow: the day was going to happen whether she wanted it to or not. Miss Kasia, her former dance teacher in Calgary, had always said to just go out and have fun, no matter what.

"I'll certainly try," she said to herself as she headed to the kitchen.

"Ready for today?" Dad asked as he handed Juliana her plate: half a grapefruit, four strips of bacon, two hash browns, and a generous helping of scrambled eggs. "Trucker's food," he said with a grin.

When she was young, Juliana would sometimes spend PD days in Dad's truck on short-haul trips. Now that she was fourteen, schoolwork and dance had replaced those days. She also rarely ate truck-stop food anymore: as a competitive dancer, she couldn't afford to eat anything that sapped her of her energy. Dad sometimes brought home some of the wonderfully greasy food anyway, almost like an apology for being away so often. This morning, though, Juliana couldn't tell if Dad was apologizing in advance of his first drive since the family's move across the country, or if he was wishing her good luck for her first day at her new school.

Whatever it was, Juliana wasn't sure her nerves would let her eat. She stared at her plate, though the smells and memories were urging her to shovel it in as fast as possible.

"You have to eat, sweetie," Mom said. "You'll have a hard time getting through the day if you don't." She carried her dishes to the sink.

Today was Mom's first full day at her new job, too. She was a grocery store manager, and although this had been her career for as long as Juliana could remember, it was a new store for her. Was Mom nervous, too? Before Juliana could ask, Mom had already disappeared into the bathroom to finish getting ready.

Once Juliana got the first bite of hash browns down her throat, her stomach settled and she wolfed down the delicious comfort food.

Footsteps coming up the creaky stairs signalled Opa's arrival in the kitchen.

"Oh my," he said. "My kitchen hasn't smelled this wonderful in years!"

"Here you go, Peter," Dad said as he passed Opa a plate.

Opa sat at the spot Mom had just vacated. "Today is your first day of school, right?"

Juliana had stuffed her mouth fuller than a chipmunk's, so she could only nod.

"Are you excited?"

Before Juliana could answer, Mom came rushing back into the kitchen, her coat now in hand.

"I've gotta go," she said. "I don't want to be late." She kissed Juliana on the cheek and Juliana immediately wiped that spot with her sleeve.

"Mom! I'm fourteen!"

"Young girls don't like that," Opa said to his daughter. "Your mom never did that to your sister's kids."

Mom shot them both a look. "Sometimes a mother's love is overflowing. Anyways," she continued to Juliana, "good luck with today. I won't be home until tonight. Anne will be by to cook, okay? But I'll be home in time to take you to dance this evening."

Juliana nodded, and Mom rushed to the landing by the side door and slipped into her boots. "Bye, everyone!" She closed the door behind her.

"I remember my first day of school," Opa said. "I was seven."

Dad, who had been eating at the stove this entire time, said, "Sorry, Peter, but we've got to hurry, too. I have to visit the principal with Juliana, and he asked that we come in before the bell. And since Katy has the car, we're walking."

"Oh, of course," Opa said. His face looked momentarily

sad, but he seemed to shake it off. "I'll save the story for later," he said and continued eating.

After breakfast, Juliana brushed her teeth, inspected her school bag to make sure everything was packed neatly in its place, and headed out with Dad.

FIRST PERIOD WAS HALFWAY THROUGH BY THE TIME JULIANA and Dad had finished in the principal's office. Mr. B.—that's what he said everyone called him because no one could remember his last name—had reviewed Juliana's next few weeks. Her old school was on a term system, with eight classes for most of the year, but her new one was on a semester system. This created a bit of a bind for Juliana. She would have to study exceptionally hard over the next few weeks so that she could write three exams: physical education & health, French, and art. And to catch up to her classmates who would be writing four exams, Juliana would have to take a class in the summer.

Way to ruin my first summer here, she thought.

Dad left to take a cab to his new trucking company, and Juliana walked alone to her health class. When she found the right classroom, she stopped outside the door, nervous to the moon and back. *I can't shake it out, I'll look stupid*, she thought, though not being able to move added to her stress. She knew everyone would be staring at her when she entered and that she would have to sit wherever there was an empty desk, meaning there was a good chance she wouldn't be able to hide in the back. She stared at her boots. In her mind, she could hear Rachel encouraging her to just knock and go in. "Sometimes you've just got to deal with it," Rachel would say. "You'll be fine. Don't worry!"

Juliana took a deep breath, knocked, and saw heads turn toward her. She opened the door and stepped inside.

"Juliana?" the teacher asked. "Welcome! I'm Ms. Haseltine."

Juliana couldn't quite tell if Ms. Haseltine was the gym teacher or a young assistant: She didn't look much older than Juliana's cousin Rebecca, and she wore loose-fitting khakis, hiking shoes, a baggy t-shirt, and had her hair pulled up in a ponytail.

Juliana saw the full sea of expressionless faces staring at her. *Crap. Something's wrong with me. My hair?* she thought.

"The class is pretty full, so we just have this one empty desk." Ms. Haseltine pointed to a desk in the front corner.

"Everyone, this is Juliana Roth. She just moved here from Calgary. Can we give her a big welcome?" Ms. Haseltine could've jumped out of one of those movies about an inspirational teacher who by the end triumphantly reaches even the most delinquent students. But Juliana wasn't at the end of that movie yet—so far the teacher's enthusiasm only made things more awkward.

The class responded with a monotone "hi."

"That wasn't a big hello!" Ms. Haseltine said, the energy in her voice trying to make up for the lack of joy in the class.

"Hi," Juliana said quickly to avoid forcing the class to fake another greeting. She walked across the room to her desk.

"Exam time," Ms. Haseltine said apologetically.

Maybe you're just weird, Juliana thought as Ms. Haseltine returned to her lesson.

Juliana pulled a notebook and pen out of her bag, opened it, and began to take notes. The topics for review today focused on safety and fitness. She hadn't learned much of the content in her health class at her old school, so she scribbled like mad to keep up.

Juliana walked home with her winter jacket open. The wet cold that marked winters in Southern Ontario was uncomfortable, but she had dressed too warmly for today's weather. At least, though, her fingers wouldn't freeze while she talked to Dad.

"I sat alone at lunch," she told him.

"That's normal," Dad replied, his voice tinny on the speaker phone in his truck.

"But couldn't they at least have some kind of student buddy for the day? That's what we always did in Calgary."

She turned down a street. Her school was only a fifteen-minute walk from home, and she was already halfway there.

"So you could be stuck with someone you can't stand? Remember when that happened to Rachel in grade seven?"

Dad had a point. "I guess. But if it was the right person, then I would've had a new friend already."

"Stop worrying about it—this will pass. You're a bright, beautiful, and friendly young lady. You'll find your friends."

"How do you know? You're not a teen."

"Are we starting that again? You act as though your mother and I have forgotten what it was like to be your age."

"It was different back then. You had no Internet."

"We didn't grow up in the Dark Ages, either. We were still teens attending high school. And for the record, I got Internet access when I was sixteen. So, how was the rest of your day?"

"I don't know," she said. "I have so much to learn in only a few weeks." She explained that she had spent the fourth period in what Mr. B. called "credit recovery," where she had to learn whatever she hadn't learned in Calgary in French and art.

"I know you, sweetheart," Dad said. "You'll get through it."

Juliana didn't want to talk about it anymore if all she

was going to get was lame attempts at motivation. "Where are you now?" she asked, trying to change the subject.

"Buffalo."

"How far away is that?"

"Just over the border, not quite three hours away. Listen, sweetie, your mom and I care a lot about you. This is just one day out of the next three-and-a-half years. Trust me. You'll find new friends faster than you think."

There was another quiet pause. Juliana hated her dad's job: it kept him away from his family for far too long. This time, he'd be gone for five days.

"I've gotta get going," Dad said. "The traffic is really starting to pile up here. I need to stay focused. But you can call me later, okay? If I can't answer, leave me a message and I'll call you back. Got it?"

"Sure thing," Juliana said.

Dad hung up just as she reached the front door. Day one of her new life was only halfway over. Despite its less-than-stellar beginning, she at least had her evening at the dance studio to look forward to.

CHAPTER TWO

*N*ine-year old Anna stood in the doorway between the kitchen and the front room. "I've scrubbed the potatoes," she said. "Now what?"

Elisabeth rolled her eyes, her back fortunately turned to her sister. She puffed out a sheet over Luki's bed and let it float on to the mattress.

"Peel them," she said, trying hard to sound calm. *Even Jesus couldn't have had this much patience*, she thought.

"And where do I put the peel?"

Elisabeth stamped her foot and turned around, only to catch an evil grin on Anna's face. Her sister, often shy around strangers, and usually preferring a logical answer over an emotional one, was far from a saint when she didn't want to do what she was supposed to do.

Which right now was to make a chicken and vegetable soup for lunch.

"You know *exactly* where to put the peel, and you can take the slop pail out to the animals when you're done. Jesus spared our lives last week. You could at least pretend to be grateful for it!"

Anna assumed a smug look and then sauntered back into the kitchen to continue her work. The year 1920 had had a difficult start for the Schuhmachers: the family had just survived the influenza that was travelling through their Romanian village, though some families were not so lucky and had lost someone, often a young child. Other families were still sick, and there might possibly be still more deaths to come.

After days of washing and scrubbing all the linens by hand, Elisabeth could finally put fresh sheets on their beds in the front room, one of three rooms in their home. In the middle was the kitchen, and on its other side was the back room, the formal room in the house. Built onto the rear of the house was an above-ground cold-storage cellar, followed by the summer kitchen, which had been divided to make room for the family's shoemaking workshop. Behind that were the stalls for the horses and cows, and then came the outhouse.

After she tucked in the sheet on Luki's bed, Elisabeth turned around and caught sight of the figure of Jesus on the crucifix over the door.

"I'm sorry for my anger," she whispered to Jesus. "Thank you for helping us through these tough times."

The house door in the kitchen flew open, letting in a wintry breeze, before slamming shut.

"Elisabeth!" Luki yelled.

Already forgetting her desire to show her siblings more patience, Elisabeth let out an exasperated "What?"

Her young brother stayed standing at the door, remembering not to come in where the snow on his boots would melt into the dirt-and-chaff floor. With their father gone to America to earn money, eight-year-old Luki now spent time every day with Mammi in the workshop, learning how to make shoes.

"Mammi needs food," Luki said. "But just a little."

"Rosina, can you please help Luki? I'm still making the beds."

From where she sat at the table in the front room, trying to knit, Rosina said, "No!" The youngest in the family at only six, she didn't hesitate to refuse her sister's orders. Unlike Anna, who dragged her disobedience out, Rosina simply got straight to the point.

"You've been allowed to knit for the past hour," Elisabeth said. "Now please help your family."

Rosina sighed, threw her single row of knitting onto the table, and stomped into the kitchen.

Elisabeth groaned inwardly at Rosina's reaction as she spread a crocheted blanket and then a down-filled comforter on Luki's bed. She moved to the next bed, reached into an open seam in the mattress, and pushed the straw around to even it out.

Because Herr Blum—Luki and Anna's school teacher—had caught the flu himself this week, Elisabeth would have to manage with all her siblings all day for the week, and it was only Monday morning.

She glanced up again at Jesus. "You will help me, won't You?"

ELISABETH STOOD AT THE CERAMIC WASHING BOWL IN THE kitchen.

"Just one more trip, please, Anna," she said as she handed Anna the slop pail filled with dirty, soapy water. Anna needed to dump the pail in the pigs' trough and then refill the washing bowl from the well in the yard. "We've only got a few plates left, but the water is too dirty for me to finish them."

Anna dragged her feet over to the door.

"The longer you take, the less time you'll have to do your embroidery."

Anna leaned to one side to compensate for the pail's weight. "Maybe I don't want to do embroidery today!"

Elisabeth rolled her eyes. "Then do something else! But I have to teach you how to iron this afternoon, and then we need to prepare supper. If you want a short break, hurry up!"

Not heeding what Elisabeth said, Anna moved at a snail's pace.

"God will strike you dead by the time you reach the well!" Elisabeth said.

"Anna's going to die?" Rosina cried out from the front room. She burst into tears.

Elisabeth rushed over to her sister and stroked her head. "No, she won't. It's just an expression. Anna will be fine." Then she glowered at Anna, who still stood at the door, wearing a satisfied grin.

Anna finally did move her feet faster, and by the time she returned, Elisabeth had managed to calm Rosina down and to explain that she'd meant Anna would get old and die if she took too long. But judging by the look on her sister's face, Rosina still didn't understand. To distract her instead, Elisabeth asked Rosina to help with the last few dishes.

Elisabeth picked up the bar of soap she had made several weeks before, rubbed it on her washcloth, and washed another plate. She dipped the plate several times to rinse it, trying to keep her hand out of the cold water, and handed it to Anna to dry, who then handed it to Rosina to put away. Within ten minutes, the girls had the remaining dishes finished.

"You can go and do what you choose," Elisabeth said.

Their moods instantly changed and they ran into the front room.

Elisabeth dumped the water into the now empty slop pail and washed out the washing bowl with her cloth. Satisfied that everything was in place, she took a short break herself and joined her sisters. Now that she was finally getting used to running the household while Mammi took care of Tata's shoemaking business, Elisabeth could afford to sit down for a few minutes throughout the day and still complete her chores before bedtime.

Rosina had returned to her knitting and Anna had taken up some embroidery. Elisabeth pulled out Tata's letter, which had arrived the week before. The family had waited for almost two months for word of his arrival in America when this letter finally came. Anna asked immediately if Elisabeth could read the letter to them again. Both sisters stopped their handiwork and looked at Elisabeth as she read:

Dear Lissa, Lissika, Anna, Luki, and Rosina,

I have arrived safely in Harrisburg, Pennsylvania. I have found work in a cigar factory. It stinks so much that I ask the other men I live with to not smoke when I'm home. It's embarrassing to have to make such a request. But the job is a good one and will allow me to save up money for our new roof and, I hope, a dowry for Elisabeth. The days are long, and I'm tired when my shift is over, but I still make and repair shoes. Sometimes it is in exchange for food, but food is also pay, isn't it? I hope to return within a year, as I said before I left. But if that is not possible, then before Elisabeth marries.

May God bless you all,

Your Tata

ROSINA AND ANNA'S EYES WELLED UP. ELISABETH SMILED AT them, placed the letter in a special box she kept atop the large cabinet in the front room, and then opened her arms, inviting her sisters into an embrace.

"Tata will be back," she said. "But in the meantime, we must help Mammi as much as we can."

The sisters pulled back, nodded, wiped their eyes, and returned to their activities.

"Rosina, I need the scissors!" Anna shouted at her sister not a minute later.

"I need them! My end is too long and it's bothering me!" Elisabeth sighed.

"THAT'S RIGHT," ELISABETH SAID TO ANNA AS SHE WATCHED her sister gently push the iron up and down a pair of Luki's pants. "Now, keep that crease flat." Luki's pants, like all men's pants, were made from two widths of linen that had been spun and woven at home. The pants therefore needed several pleats to make them narrower, and it was Elisabeth's job to ensure their creases were clean and crisp.

Someone knocked at the house door and Anna immediately left the iron on the fabric and ran to answer it. Elisabeth sighed as she picked up the iron and placed it on the stove for safety.

Into the kitchen walked Omama, Mammi's mother, and Peter-Bátschi, Mammi's brother.

"Anna, fetch Luki and Mammi," Elisabeth said, and Anna said hello to her grandmother and uncle, slipped on some boots, and ran around the back of the house to the workshop without a complaint.

Of course she does what I ask when an adult is here, Elisabeth thought.

Rosina hid behind Elisabeth's skirt, and peeked out at her grandmother.

Omama was a short, stocky woman. She was among the oldest in the village—in her sixties—a position that was confirmed by her sitting at the front of church every Sunday with other elders. She wore a dress with dark blue fabric covered with a patterned print of tiny ovals. The dress buttoned up the bodice and closed at the base of Omama's neck, and a black apron covered the bottom half. Over her hair she wore a headscarf that tied under her chin, with the edge of her white *haube* just peeking out from underneath.

Elisabeth pulled out a chair for her grandmother to sit on while she removed her boots and put on her house shoes.

The house door opened again as Luki and Mammi entered.

"Where is my little man of the house?" Omama asked.

Luki ran into her open arms.

"I hope you are looking after your family?"

Actually, I am, Elisabeth thought.

Luki nodded eagerly. "Mammi's showing me how to make shoes!"

Omama nodded in approval. "You will be a man some-day, Luki. It's a shame your father has left at such a time."

Luki frowned.

Was that comment really necessary? Elisabeth thought.

"Modr," Mammi said as she kissed her mother on each cheek. "Peter. What brings you here?"

Only now did Elisabeth notice how embarrassed Peter-Bátschi looked: his cheeks were flushed and aside from quick hellos, he kept his eyes focused on the ground.

"I am tired of picking up after my son and his wife," Omama began. Omama lived with Peter-Bátschi and his family. Her mouth turned upside down and her eyes narrowed into slits as she glared up at her son. "He was at Tiny Hay's on Friday afternoon again and didn't come home until after *I* had fed the animals."

Tiny Hay was the nickname for Hay Heinrich, whose

great-grandfather had been a very short man. Hay Heinrich actually had a fairly average build for a farmer, but once a person had been given a nickname by the community, that name would be passed down through the family.

Elisabeth's uncle looked up, though he showed very little confidence. "Tiny Hay was talking about his cousin, one of the two prisoners of war who had just arrived from Russia." Elisabeth had seen the men at church yesterday and had witnessed the tight embraces and numerous kisses they had received before the service. The men looked familiar to her, but she couldn't remember their names. One was missing three-quarters of an arm. Mammi had discreetly slapped Elisabeth on the leg to stop her from staring. The other man had looked healthy. *That must be who Peter-Bátschi's talking about*, she thought and regretted that she had spent so much time at home that she didn't know what was happening in the village.

Peter-Bátschi's attempt to defend himself was in vain. "You always have an excuse," Omama said. "Last week it was about those whatever-they're-called in Russia."

"Bolsheviks," Peter-Bátschi said.

"What do they have to do with your life?"

"Well, nothing, I suppose, but—"

To Elisabeth's dismay, Omama wouldn't let her son get a word in edgewise. One thing Elisabeth missed about her father's absence was the men's conversations, and it looked like this was as close to one as she was going to get.

"Leave Russia alone, and leave the war alone. I don't need to hear that kind of talk in my house," Omama said.

For a moment, Elisabeth felt pity for her grandmother: Adam-Bátschi and Andreas-Bátschi, two of Mammi's brothers, had died in the war. *I wouldn't want to talk about the war every day either*, Elisabeth thought.

But Omama charged on with her accusations against her son's family. "And your wife? She hasn't cleaned her floor in weeks, won't discipline her children, and insists she's too tired to keep on top of everything." To emphasize her point, Omama let out a quiet grunt.

Peter-Bátschi returned his gaze to the floor.

Omama shook her head. "I have tried and tried to make the children do what I say but no amount of punishment would work with them. And with school cancelled for two of the children, the other two refuse to go, too. It's horrible in that house. There is no respect in that family for the elders!"

Omama's story didn't surprise Elisabeth. She knew her uncle preferred to play *skat*, a card game, and to drink with other men whenever he was home. Over the winter, that was often. She also knew her five cousins to be an unruly bunch. Mammi complained it was because Sophie-Néni didn't discipline them enough and had therefore let the Devil in.

Mammi didn't bat an eyelash. "Make them kneel in the corn," she said matter-of-factly. "Not even Elisabeth's too old for that. She had fallen asleep while looking after the children and then dared speak back at me for demanding too much of her." She nodded in approval at her own decision. "Elisabeth hasn't fallen asleep or spoken back to me since."

Elisabeth's face grew hot. She had been working very hard at that time: helping with wedding preparations for her cousin, guiding her sisters in their chores, caring for Luki while he was sick. She was certain that even Jesus needed rest once in a while.

"That's what I said," Omama said. "I said that my daughter, Lissa, knows how to discipline." She threw an angry glance in her son's direction. "My oldest son—my *only* son now—doesn't and is embarrassing the family." She stood up and hobbled to the kitchen table. "Bring it here," she commanded him.

Peter-Bátschi reached behind the chair and pulled out a small suitcase Elisabeth hadn't noticed. Omama directed him to carry it to the back room, and he obliged.

"I am staying here until that house is cleaned and Peter learns to look after his chores," Omama declared.

Anna and Rosina all stared in fear, something Elisabeth would also have done were it not for her role as their caregiver now. Mammi's face showed little emotion, and Elisabeth tried to copy her. After what Omama had just said, she had to look like she was in control of everyone. Otherwise, she knew, there would be consequences.

CHAPTER THREE

Juliana looked at the time on her computer: 5:02. Which meant it was 3:02 in Calgary. Rachel wouldn't be home from school yet.

She stared at her notes. How was she going to get all this information into her head? Her new class had spent the entire month of November learning a mental health unit while she only had two weeks to learn it before the exam.

"This couldn't be more unfair," she said to herself as she began to make study notes from her class notes. Her only other option would be to take two courses during the summer but having to take one was already bad enough.

Juliana opened her great-grandmother's book and flipped through the drawings. *If only I could dance like she could draw*, Juliana thought. She turned to a drawing near the front again, a picture of the back of an envelope about to be opened. She wondered what could be so important about an envelope that had compelled Omama to draw it.

Slow footsteps down the hallway interrupted her thoughts: Opa was coming. Unlike Mom and Dad, he never knocked before entering her room, but his footsteps always announced his presence.

He poked his head into her room. "Yulika," he said, using his nickname for her. "Annie won't be coming for supper tonight. Sophie and little Scott are both sick. Stomach flu."

Annie was Mom's sister, Aunt Anne to Juliana. Of the three Schuhmacher siblings, she was the one with the big family: six kids.

"That's too bad." Secretly, Juliana half-wished they'd come over so she could catch their bug and have an excuse to not study all this material.

As Opa shuffled back down the hall, Juliana realized that this meant Aunt Anne would not be cooking supper. With Dad away and Mom at work, that left Juliana to prepare the meal. However, of all the tasks Juliana was ever asked to do in the house, the absolute worst was anything in the kitchen. *Or I could study*, she thought.

She stuck her head into the hall. "Opa, I'll cook us something."

Opa turned around and shook his head. "It's all right. I

know you have to study. We've got cereal and milk. We'll be fine."

But Juliana knew that one of the reasons the Roths had moved to Kitchener in the first place was that unless Aunt Anne came to cook, Opa would eat only cereal and milk, or summer sausage sandwiches. He had never learned how to cook, not even after Oma had died, and any attempts to hire a meal delivery service had been met with a stubborn refusal. Or so Mom had said. But as soon as they had moved in, Mom had insisted on the service. Aunt Anne offered to continue cooking for another two weeks, allowing Juliana's parents to adjust to their new lives and Opa to adjust to his new cooks. After that, she could focus on her family again.

That didn't help with tonight, though, and Juliana needed something more nutritious than cereal before dance. She closed her laptop and followed Opa out to the kitchen.

"It's time for a break for me, anyway."

"All right. I'll just be downstairs," he said. "I don't want to miss the six o'clock news."

"But Opa, it's just past five."

"All the more reason to hurry. There's this big story in the newspaper about rubber workers and I don't want to miss it," he said and headed to his room in the basement, leaving Juliana confused. What did the newspaper have to do with missing the news on TV? Or was that just a slip of the tongue? But if it was, was he always this worried about being late for something? Because she didn't know her grandfather well, she had a hard time telling what was dementia and what was just his personality.

Juliana opened the fridge and surveyed her possible ingredients and then checked the freezer, where she found a frozen apple core. Had Opa left it there?

"Now you're being paranoid," she said to herself as she took it out and threw in the green bin. "You've put a box of cereal in the fridge before." But deep down, she wasn't so sure.

BACK FROM DANCE THAT NIGHT, JULIANA AND MOM TOOK their boots off at the landing by the side door.

"I'm sorry," Mom said. "Your first day of school and then you're left to cook on top of that. We should figure out another plan."

"It was just this one evening, no big deal. We had tons of food, so I found something for us." She grabbed an apple and a handful of almonds and sat down at the table. Mom followed suit.

"Listen, Juliana," she said, "I'm afraid much of this week is going to look like today. I'll be home to drive you, but I think I'll be working at least sixty hours this week."

Juliana's shoulders drooped. "Seriously? Your first week

on the job and you can't work even just, you know, like regular people?"

Mom put her apple on the table. "The place is an absolute mess. I've got workers who don't care an ounce about their jobs, there was mouldy produce almost everywhere I looked, the floors are dirty because the cleaning company rarely shows up with a full complement of staff, and I found a whole pallet of flour sitting outside. Thankfully, that company knew how to package it so bugs couldn't get in, but no one wanted to move it. So, yes, it's going to be like that."

"Great. So I'm cooking all week? When I have to get ready for exams? I've got so much to learn, I don't know how I'm going to get it all done."

Mom shook her head. "No, of course you're not cooking all week. Stop being so dramatic. I'll use my lunch break tomorrow to bring home some food you can just throw in the oven if Anne can't make it tomorrow or Wednesday. I'm off Thursday, and your dad's back on Friday."

But Juliana knew it wouldn't happen that way. Every time her parents said it would be fine, it wasn't. Too tired to debate it further, though, she grabbed her snack and bag and dragged her tired feet to her room.

"Good night," Mom called after her.

"Yeah," Juliana replied and closed her bedroom door behind her. She looked at herself in her full-length mirror.

"I have to go to school, study, dance, and practice. And guess who's also going to have to cook?"

Just then, her phone beeped. She picked it up and let out a little squeal. Rachel!

You forgot to call, Rachel wrote, referring to Juliana's promise from a few days ago.

Sorry! Not my fault. Cousins sick, aunt couldn't cook. Had to make supper for me and Opa. Then dance. Just got home now.

Juliana watched the three dots fade in and out as Rachel typed.

Makes sense. Can you talk now?

No—Mom'll hear me. But I can text.

Kk. How was school?

That was all Juliana needed to unleash a flurry of words to describe in detail how lost she felt.

And it's only day 1 😞

But then Rachel texted exactly what Juliana needed to hear.

Head's up. You've got this.

The two kept texting for almost two hours. By the time they had finished, Juliana felt both better and worse: better because Rachel knew just how to talk to her to make her feel better, and worse because Rachel wasn't in Kitchener. Juliana finally dropped into a deep sleep after midnight, still in her clothes.

On only six hours of sleep, Juliana didn't know if she was going to make it through the day. As she sat in health class, Ms. Haseltine droning on and on about how to stay safe when practicing sports, Juliana's eyes began to close. The girl next to her kept shifting in her chair, as though she was the princess and the pea was under one of the chair's legs. As annoying as it was to see, the girl's jitters kept Juliana awake, but just barely.

Juliana began doodling in her notebook, unable to focus on the material Ms. Haseltine was teaching.

I am definitely not an artist, she thought as she stared at the grade-two-level stick figure she'd drawn. *That gene did not get passed down to me.* She tried to draw a basic envelope, but her rendition of it looked more like a collection of misshapen triangles instead. Juliana attempted to shade in her lop-sided creation, like Omama had, but nothing she tried could come even close to the envelope depicted in the old book. As her mind drifted off to wondering more about her great-grandmother's life, her head sank onto her arms, the sound of Ms. Haseltine's voice disappearing into the background.

A gentle shaking awoke Juliana, and she lifted her head. The girl sitting next to her smiled.

"Tired?" she whispered.

Juliana looked around. No one was staring at her, but maybe they had already done that. She sat up and then noticed in horror at the little mark of drool on her notebook. She tried to discreetly cover it up, but the girl next to her had probably noticed it. However, the expression on her face told Juliana she wouldn't tell anyone.

Juliana returned to her doodling and head nodding as her brain tried to drag her back to sleep. Today was going to be absolute torture.

Juliana unlocked the door to her home and entered. She couldn't wait to fall into her bed for a nap. She left her boots by the landing and headed up into the kitchen to hang her jacket in the hallway closet.

"Yulika?" Opa called from the basement.

"Yeah?" she replied, hoping Opa wouldn't launch into a long story.

As Opa walked up the stairs, Juliana grabbed herself a tangerine and began to peel it. Opa appeared, a huge smile on his face.

"How was school?"

"Good," she replied, not really wanting to say much else.

"Better than yesterday?"

Juliana shrugged. "Someone smiled at me, so I guess, yeah." She turned around and noticed that Opa's buttons weren't matched to the proper buttonholes, with several holes skipped altogether.

Juliana wasn't sure if she should say something. She didn't want to embarrass Opa, and so long as he wasn't leaving the house, he'd probably be fine. Or would he be embarrassed later after realizing it himself and wondering how long his shirt had been like that? Opa followed her gaze before she could decide what to say.

"Oh, my," he said, somewhat embarrassed, and Juliana blushed, too. "Looks like I had a problem today." He laughed, but it was a laugh Juliana now associated with Opa pretending as though nothing was wrong. She smiled back because she didn't know what else to do.

To her surprise, Opa unbuttoned his shirt right in front of her, revealing his white undershirt. Juliana looked away, unsure if this was part of his dementia or whether he'd just gotten used to dressing anywhere in the house because he had lived alone for so long. Although she hadn't seen him do this before, it had only been three weeks since the Roths had moved in.

"I'm pretty tired," she said, facing her tangerine. "I had a late night."

"But you haven't told me everything about your day yet. It's nice to hear that someone smiled at you!"

Juliana turned to face Opa again, and this time, his buttons matched up. "Maybe at supper?" she asked. "Please? I really need to sleep."

Opa nodded and Juliana headed back to her room,

happy to get out of the awkward situation. Her phone beeped, so she pulled it out of her backpack.

How was today? It was Mom.

Fine, Juliana texted back.

Anything important happen?

Juliana debated whether she should tell Mom about Opa's shirt, but her bed looked so inviting. Even her thumbs felt like five-kilogram weights.

Lots to do. Gotta go.

There was a pause, and them Mom texted, *Ok.*

Juliana set her alarm and tucked herself in.

CHAPTER FOUR

The following morning, Mammi said she didn't need Luki. Elisabeth couldn't very well have him do household chores, but she didn't want him playing while she and her sisters cleaned. If the senior school—the one responsible for grades three to six—was closed for the week, then Elisabeth would have to step in as her siblings' teacher. That would help keep them occupied, sitting at one table for a good hour or two.

"'But when the morning was now come,'" Elisabeth read from the Bible to her siblings in the front room, "'Jesus stood on the shore: but the disciples knew not that it was Jesus.'"

"This is boring," Luki said.

"Would you say that to Herr Blum?" Elisabeth asked.

"You're not Herr Blum," Anna answered. "You're not a teacher. This is boring. I want to embroider."

"I want to knit!" Rosina added.

Elisabeth took a deep breath and let it out slowly while she prayed to Jesus for patience. How was she ever going to make it through this week? "But you need to continue with your schooling. How else are you going to learn to read and do math?"

Omama hobbled out of the back room, dressed in a dark dress with a dainty floral pattern on it, her hair covered by her *haube* and a dark headscarf. She pulled up a chair in the front room and sat down. Shivers ran down Elisabeth's spine.

"Elisabeth," Omama said, "my dress from yesterday needs washing. It's in the back room."

"Yes, Omama. I'll add it my laundry work." Elisabeth turned her attention back to the children. "We're going to continue. This is an important story from the Bible. 'Then Jesus saith unto them, Children, have ye any meat? And they answer him, No.'" Omama's frown had apparently stayed on from last night. Not sure if Omama was displeased with something in particular or everything in general, and too scared to ask lest she was expected to know the answer, Elisabeth continued. "'And he said unto—'"

"I should be helping Mammi," Luki said, his mouth also in a deep frown.

"I need to learn how to knit," Rosina said, her arms crossed.

"And how am I going to be a good wife if I can't embroider?" Anna asked.

Was it just Elisabeth, or were her siblings trying to get out of reading by saying things they knew Omama would like to hear? Elisabeth took another deep breath. Omama was here because of how horrible it was to live at Peter-Bátschi's house, and Elisabeth didn't want to embarrass Mammi by allowing her siblings to be disobedient. She had to keep them under control.

"This story is important," she explained to Anna. "It's about having faith in the Lord."

"But I already have faith," Anna stated.

Luki stood up. "Mammi doesn't read in the workshop, so why do I need to sit here?"

"Because Mammi asked you to," Elisabeth reminded him.

"She didn't say I had to read." He crossed his arms over his chest and turned his lips upside down into a pout.

Omama wagged a finger at Luki. "You listen to your sister."

Elisabeth was shocked. Omama was actually supporting her decision to make the children sit and learn?

"No!" Luki replied.

Omama's face turned red faster than God struck down

people. "Your sister has many faults, but she is in charge of the household."

"I am the man of the house," Luki said. "You even said so yesterday!"

"The man of the house knows when to listen to his wife. You don't have one, and your mother is working, so that person is your sister."

It wasn't about reading, Elisabeth now realized. It was about listening to her.

Impatient and now angry, Luki dashed for the kitchen but came too close to Omama. She grabbed him by the arm and gave him a strong wallop on the bottom. Luki immediately began to cry.

"That is how you make your siblings behave," Omama instructed Elisabeth.

Tears streaming down his face, Luki slumped back into his chair. Elisabeth reached out to him, but Omama tapped the table to get her attention.

"You are in charge of this household," she said. "You are not his friend. Now, continue with your reading."

Elisabeth glanced at Anna and Rosina, who both looked scared. Elisabeth hoped they knew she would never do that to them, just like she could never spank Luki, no matter how disobedient he was. Something inside her told her that Jesus wouldn't do that, either.

THE REST OF THE MORNING PASSED WITH HARDLY A WORD exchanged between the children for fear of any kind of reprisal from Omama. Elisabeth had finished teaching their lessons and even had time to show Luki how to polish shoes, though she had to make it very clear that he only had to do this when he finished making them, and not when the family prepared to leave the house. That was a woman's job. She also helped Rosina with her knitting and explained a new embroidery stitch to Anna.

After lunch, Omama retreated to the back room to lie down on the guest bed for a rest. Luki had gone out in the workshop with Mammi, who had worked through lunch to keep up with her orders. Anna stood at the washing bowl to wash the dishes while Rosina dried them. Elisabeth wrapped cloths around a plate of hot food to keep Mammi's lunch warm. She knew Mammi would ask how the animals were so before she took the food to Mammi, she stopped to check on them first.

Elisabeth started with the poultry yard beside the house, which included coops for chickens, geese, and ducks. One of the ducks looked nicely fattened.

"I'll be out for you later," she said to it.

She passed the wagon shed and *hambar*, a structure that was used to store dried corn, to reach the pigpen. As she turned to leave for the horse and cow stalls, a glint of something caught her eye.

"What's that?" she asked herself and looked closer.

Several nails lay on the ground in the pigpen, where the pigs could step or roll on them. Elisabeth slid her arm between the boards, but she couldn't quite reach the nails. She pushed her hand in farther, lost her balance, and fell into the boards. A creak and then a light snap told her something wooden had broken.

"Oh no!"

She reached the nails, pulled her arm back, and saw that the wood on the rail had splintered and that a long, deep crack now travelled down the board. Further inspecting the damage, she discovered where the nails had come from. She tried to check all six pigs, looking for any wounds. To her relief, she found none.

"If that isn't repaired soon, the pigs could break out," she said aloud, looking at the damaged boards.

A pig oinked in response.

She quickly checked the horse and cow stalls in the main barn, adding water to the trough, throwing hay into the horses' and cows' enclosures. She hurried back and picked up Mammi's lunch and then carried it into Tata's workshop. Luki looked up when she entered.

"How are the animals?" Mammi asked, not looking up from her work. Her voice sounded unusually tired. Was Omama's stay already too much for her? Elisabeth could certainly understand that.

"Fine," Elisabeth blurted out as she set the plate down. "But we have a problem."

"Oh?" Mammi still didn't look up.

Elisabeth told her what had happened.

"I'm sorry," Elisabeth finished. "I didn't want to waste time getting those nails out, so I reached in, and that's when I stumbled and broke the boards."

Mammi waved a hand at Elisabeth. "Yes, you need to be more careful, but Elisabeth, there is no way your stumbling would have damaged them so much unless they were already nearly broken."

Elisabeth breathed a sigh of relief. For once something wasn't her fault.

"But we need someone to repair them," Mammi declared.

"I can't fix it," Luki said, "because Tata never showed me how to do that."

The tone in her brother's voice angered Elisabeth: Luki was using Tata's absence as an excuse to not help out. Mammi heard it too, judging by the look on her face. She stood up from her chair at the workbench, grabbed a scrub brush, dunked it in a small pail of water she kept in the workshop, and pushed it into his hand.

"Then make yourself useful and clean up the workbench," she said. "I want this spotless by the time I return."

Luki's eyes widened in surprise and he immediately set to work while Mammi followed Elisabeth out to the stalls to take a look.

Elisabeth carried a bowl of boiled potatoes to the kitchen table, where Omama, Mammi, and Luki already sat waiting for supper. Anna set the table and then took her seat, rocking her chair as she waited, while Rosina carried over cheese, bread, and butter before kneeling on her chair. All that was needed was the duck, which Elisabeth now pulled out of the oven and set on some tea towels in the middle of the table.

"Elisabeth, get me some water," Omama said, and Elisabeth obliged.

Just as Elisabeth was about to sit down, Mammi instructed her to carve the duck and serve everyone.

"But you're the head of our household," Elisabeth said, confused.

"And I've worked hard enough outside. Or are you suggesting that you work harder in here?" Mammi's accusation took Elisabeth aback. She had meant no such thing: she was just confused by the change of routine. But without saying another word, she carved the duck, placed a slice on each person's plate, and helped her siblings cut their portions.

"Mammi, I want school to start again," Anna said, rocking on her chair.

"Psht!" Mammi said. "You do not speak at the table! And sit like a woman."

Anna looked down at her plate of food. Elisabeth began slicing her own duck. Then Luki spilled his glass of water. Elisabeth raced to the back room to get tea towels and returned to find Anna rocking again.

"Anna, stop it." Why wasn't she listening? There were adults in the room. Or was she trying to get her older sister in trouble?

"It's your job to discipline her," Omama said. "You are in charge."

Elisabeth prayed that Anna would listen to her and avoid forcing an uncomfortable confrontation between Elisabeth and their grandmother. She dried Luki's spill and sat down, hoping to finally start eating, only to catch Rosina trying to pour water from the water jug. Fearing another accident, Elisabeth helped her.

"Aaahhh!" Anna screamed as her chair tipped back. Anna's head hit the ground, and Elisabeth immediately rushed to help her sister up.

"If you had sat like a woman," Mammi said, "this wouldn't have happened."

Omama nodded in agreement. "You should have listened to your mother." Neither got up to help, and Elisabeth wondered how their words helped at all. She didn't know the Bible off by heart, of course, but she could not think of a single passage where Jesus spoke that way. And was it not a Christian's duty to be like Him?

So far as Elisabeth could tell, though, Anna hadn't heard a word of it: she was wailing.

"Shh," Elisabeth said to her sister as she helped her up. "Eat the rest of your food. You'll feel better soon."

Still sniffling, Anna nodded while Elisabeth placed her chair back at the table. Anna sat down and picked at her food.

"That is no way to teach her," Omama said. "She'll only do it again."

Elisabeth's shoulders tensed. Why on earth would Anna rock her chair again after such a fall? Even if she did, a gentle reminder about her fall should be enough to deter her the next time. Elisabeth sometimes wondered if adults really did understand children the way they said they did.

Another string of requests from everyone, though, meant that by the time Elisabeth finally sat down to eat, everyone else had finished their meal. Elisabeth often counted on her meals as breaks from her endless list of chores. Hopefully Omama and Mammi would give her enough time to eat.

"Anna, Rosina, go into the front room and work on your projects. Luki, try not to be a nuisance," Mammi instructed.

"He can practice polishing shoes," Elisabeth offered.

Mammi raised her eyebrows. "A very good idea, Lissika. Luki, continue with your practice."

Luki sulked, but one look from Omama wiped it off his face. The three younger siblings disappeared into the warm room of the house and Mammi closed the door behind them.

Elisabeth's heart started to race. Had she done something wrong? Said something to embarrass her mother? Insulted Omama in some way?

Mammi stood with her back to the door and looked Omama in the eye. Elisabeth didn't think her heart could race any faster.

"We need to talk about your future," Mammi began. Elisabeth kept eating. "You turn fifteen this summer. It's time we start finding you a husband."

Elisabeth's hand with its forkful of duck froze halfway along its path to her mouth. *A husband? Am I ready for one already?*

"You still have much work to do," said Omama. "You need to stop speaking up like you do, especially the way you did at church on Christmas Eve. The Bible says, 'Let your women keep silence in the churches: for it is not permitted unto them to speak; but they are commanded to be under obedience, as also saith the law.'"

Upon hearing that verse, Elisabeth bristled. "But Krehling Maria and Wagner Anna were speaking up at a time when it was wrong to do so."

Omama wagged her crooked finger at Elisabeth. "That is for Jesus to judge, not you."

But Mammi had approved Elisabeth's speaking up: the other women had been criticizing Pastor Fröhlich's preference for Hungarian as the language of worship in the church and of instruction in the schools, though the children currently learned in Romanian as the new laws dictated. Christmas Eve was an inappropriate time to discuss such topics. Was Elisabeth supposed to stay silent and let those women disturb the sanctity of the church with a political discussion?

"Modr, Elisabeth still has much to learn," Mammi said, clearly not taking either side, at least not in front of her mother. "She has at least two years to find someone, and I will help her learn what she still needs to know."

Omama nodded and broke off a piece of bread from the loaf that still sat on the table. "Does that mean she'll learn to stop smiling so much?"

Omama's question angered Elisabeth, but she swallowed her words. Her mother had told her in the past to smile less, because otherwise people would think she looked stupid. *But smiling means someone is happy and enjoying what Jesus has blessed them with. Why should I not show that?*

"You must always be on your best behaviour," Omama said. "Just like your husband must respect you, you must respect him, and that means learning your role in the family."

Elisabeth smiled at Omama, who scowled back. Even Mammi shot her oldest child a look of mild scorn.

"Now," Mammi said, "we've invited someone to tea

tomorrow to discuss the pigpens. I expect you to be polite to him."

Maybe Mammi meant it would be a young man. Elisabeth nodded.

"Good. Get your sisters and begin cleaning up the kitchen," Mammi commanded. "Luki and I will head back to the workshop."

Mammi believed Elisabeth was ready to marry and receive her *haube*, and to have a family. Elisabeth smiled, jumped up from her chair, and called her siblings. Excitement filling her soul, she ignored Omama's comments about smiling.

CHAPTER FIVE

Juliana wiped the sweat from her brow as she and the rest of her tap group headed to the change room after a particularly intense practice.

"You all right?" Jasmine asked Juliana. "You were completely distracted in class there."

Juliana couldn't argue with her: she had forgotten parts of the choreography she and Jasmine had practiced last weekend, before school had started, and Miss Denise had had to repeat herself several times during the past two hours. Juliana knew she had a long road ahead of her to catch up to the calibre of her new team, but she was failing miserably at it today.

"Life's just really crappy right now," she confessed. "My grandfather's acting weird and my dad's on the road until

Friday. My aunt was supposed to cook for us last night but she couldn't, so I had to, and Mom's hardly home right now, too, and to top it all off, I've got to catch up on half a year's work within a couple of weeks."

When the entire group grabbed water and snacks and headed to the homework room, Jasmine held Juliana back.

"Listen. It sounds like you've got a lot going on, but the more energy you waste brooding about it, the worse it's going to get."

Jasmine's comment took Juliana aback. "I'm not brooding," she insisted. "We moved in with my grandfather to look after him, and I'm scared I'm the one who's actually going to be stuck with that job. I've never had this much schoolwork before, I'm the worst dancer on the team—don't try and tell me otherwise—and I feel like I'm completely alone here in all of this."

"What does complaining do about it?" Jasmine asked. "Either get help and fix it or stop brooding. You're not going to get through this if you complain all the time."

Now Jasmine thoroughly confused Juliana. She could be super-friendly one moment, and mean the next. Couldn't she show at least a little understanding?

"Well, it's tough and I need to talk about it to someone," Juliana said, defending her position. "I feel like I'm going to explode."

Jasmine picked up her snack, water, and schoolbooks and opened the door. "Then you'd better find a way to deal with it, because you've only got only a few weeks to do all that studying and if you explode before then, you'll fail on all fronts." She left. Juliana stood frozen to the floor in astonishment.

"Something wrong?" Mom asked as Juliana silently slipped into the car.

Juliana threw her bag into the back and strapped on her seatbelt without speaking.

"Well?" Mom said, looking over her shoulder as she backed out.

"It's nothing."

Mom shot her a concerned look before pulling out of the parking lot. "I know that tone of voice. It's not nothing."

Dance had felt particularly punishing, leaving Juliana with little energy to even begin to tell Mom about everything going wrong in her life. Add to that Jasmine's comments, and Juliana really wasn't in the mood for talking.

When they stopped at the intersection at the end of the short street, Mom studied Juliana. Once the road was clear, she turned out onto the main street. "I can tell something's bothering you. I know I've been really busy with work, but I've got time now. What's up?" Mom turned on her blinker, checked her rearview mirror, and pulled into the left-hand lane. "Is it school? Dance? Tata?"

"How about all of the above?" The words fell out of Juliana's mouth before she could clamp it shut. *Great. Now she's going to dig*, Juliana thought.

"I see. Okay, let's start with school. What's wrong there?"

Juliana adjusted her position in her seat. The tone in Mom's voice suggested she wasn't taking her seriously, but now that the conversation had started and Juliana was stuck in the car with her, she might as well say something.

"I don't know if I can handle all the work."

Mom stopped at a red light and faced Juliana. "You know how to organize yourself, so that's just what you'll have to do. You'll be fine."

"What if I don't know everything?"

"How can you know everything? Your father and I knew these three weeks weren't going to be easy, but we also knew you would pull through. If your marks drop a bit, it's fine. I promise we won't be angry with you."

Juliana had always maintained a ninety-percent average since percentages had first appeared on her report cards. She wasn't going to let this move hold her back from keeping that streak. How could Mom not understand how important this was to her? "Couldn't we have waited to move until I started grade ten?"

The light turned green.

"This job opened up for January, not July. And the pay is really good. We didn't know if another opportunity like this would come up again."

"Did you plan on leaving me alone at home a lot?"

Mom's voice got tense. "That's not fair. I knew the situation at the store was bad, but I didn't know how bad it was. We need to earn money, and if I don't turn things around, I won't have a job. Unlike school, where you can fail and still move forward, if you fail at your job, you get fired."

What was that supposed to mean? Just because Juliana would still go to grade ten regardless of her marks didn't mean her life was somehow easier. And why was money so important? What happened to all the money they would've gotten from selling everything? Surely her parents must have a stash of it in the bank now.

"But you sold our house and Dad's truck back home! Where did that money go? That was over half a million at least!"

Another red light. Mom hit the brakes hard, and both she and Juliana lurched forward.

"Just because you're fourteen doesn't mean you know everything," Mom seethed. "That includes our financial situation. Do you know how much of our mortgage we still had to pay off?"

Juliana had seen the price of the house online, and although she didn't know how much her father's truck sold for, she knew it wasn't pennies. But she hadn't thought about debt.

"No," she said meekly.

"Your father and I bought that house as an investment and we owed about two-thirds of its value when we sold. So that went to the bank. And then there's putting money away for Tata's care, because his employer went bankrupt when you were still young, so all three of us are contributing what we can, because we know the day will come when he needs more help than we can give him. And then we're also saving for university for you. Ontario is more expensive than any other province, and your education is going to cost us a lot. Then there's your dance lessons, income taxes, utilities, food, the cleaners...need I go on?"

Juliana sank down in her seat as far as her seatbelt would allow. "No."

"Good." The light turned green. "And before you make another accusation like that at me, *think* first!"

It would have helped if you'd told me all this earlier, Juliana thought.

THE NEXT DAY OF SCHOOL WASN'T MUCH OF AN improvement, and Juliana's new knowledge about her family's financial situation weighed heavily on her. But by the time she got home, she admitted to herself that she was tired of every day dragging down her spirits. Miss Kasia's words came back to her: *Just go out and have fun, no matter what.*

"To which Rachel would tell me now to just listen to Miss Kasia," Juliana said out loud. She smacked herself in the forehead. "Great. Now I'm having conversations with myself." But maybe lightening up a little would help her. She unlocked the side door to Opa's house, vowing to leave her stress on the driveway.

"I'm home, Opa!" she called down the stairs as she took off her boots. The door to his bedroom squeaked open and he appeared at the bottom, properly dressed. He walked upstairs as Juliana headed into the kitchen. He had had no problems conversing that morning, had put everything in its spot, and had even avoided starting any long stories while the rest of the family was in a hurry to get out the door. And now, Juliana couldn't see any signs that he was having any difficulties. If those issues before were just memory blips, then they couldn't have been serious ones. *And maybe that's just what he's like*, she thought.

She tossed her bag into her room before coming back for a snack. She poured a glass of water, found a tangerine, and sat down.

"How was today?" he asked.

"The best day so far," she said and then took a sip. "Still

no one to eat with. My phys ed teacher is a bit weird, but I think I'm getting used to her. How about you?"

"Mine was *besser als sonst*," he replied. After seeing the look of confusion on her face, he said, "Sorry. Sometimes it just slips out. Your mother's used to it." Was mixing languages another sign of his dementia? "And before you think it's because of my brain, it's not," he said, as though he could read her mind. "If you came out to the German club, you'd hear all of us older folks talking Denglish."

"Talking what?" Now he was making up words?

"Denglish. *Deutsch* plus English. Denglish."

Juliana nodded. It sounded plausible, though a bit strange. "So, what did you say?" she asked and took another sip of water.

"My day was better than usual. Doctor called today and said my urine test came out fine again."

Juliana choked on her water, and Opa's expression turned to one of concern.

"Are you all right?" He patted her on the back, and she waved her hand, signalling she didn't need the assistance.

"I'm fine, Opa. That's, um, just not the kind of thing you talk about with grandkids."

Opa patted her on the back again, but this time in a friendly manner instead of a lifesaving one. "You'll realize when you get old that there are some things you don't care about anymore, like table manners, and some things you do, like getting tested for diseases that old people get."

Juliana couldn't help but smile. "But I still care about table manners, Opa."

After her snack and a little more chitchat with her grandfather, Juliana returned to her room, feeling a bit happier. She pulled out her French books, but as she studied her irregular verbs, her mind kept wandering back to Opa and the symptoms she'd witnessed over the past few weeks. For example, he sometimes abruptly ended their conversation because he remembered something. And there was that one time he thought he was back in Semlak and told Juliana she needed to start looking for a husband because she was fourteen. Now the shirt and the apple core...Juliana's concerns distracted her enough that she eventually went online to look up Opa's symptoms. The more she read, the more concerned she became.

"This can't be right," she said to herself. "I have half the symptoms myself: forgetting, having a hard time learning stuff..." She looked at the clock on her laptop screen. "Heck, I can't even concentrate to learn the new stuff and remember it, and I know I've misplaced things. How is that any different from Opa?"

A knock at the side door to the house interrupted her thoughts and her attempt at studying. As she stepped out of her room, she heard Opa greeting Aunt Anne, Dean, and Charlie. Dean was exactly Juliana's age, but they had very little if anything in common, and Charlie was three years older and almost finished high school.

Juliana was shocked to see Charlie wearing a sleeveless basketball jersey.

"Aren't you cold?" she asked.

"No," he replied and traipsed into the kitchen. The weather was certainly warmer winter weather than Juliana was used to, but even she wore long sleeves or a sweater.

"Stomach bug over," Aunt Anne announced. "Rebecca's cooking for Tony and Scott, and the three of us are tonight's cooking brigade!"

Juliana was relieved to not have to cook or eat the packaged junk Mom had brought home.

"Where's Sophie?" she asked.

Aunt Anne handed Juliana her coat. "At climbing lessons. There's no snow outside, so she can't go skiing."

"There's nowhere to ski here, snow or no snow," Juliana said.

"There's Chicopee," Aunt Anne replied.

"The garbage dump Mom told me about?"

Aunt Anne laughed. "No, but everyone thinks that. The garbage dump is where Tata used to take us to go sledding: Mount Trashmore. Remember that, Tata?"

"What was that?" he asked.

"Mount Trashmore," Aunt Anne said.

Opa still looked confused.

CHAPTER SIX

Semlak had about five thousand people living in its streets: Romanians, Germans, Slovaks, Jews, Gypsies, Serbians, and a few other groups. From those, the Christian population worshipped at one of five churches: Greek Catholic, Roman Catholic, Orthodox, Calvinist, and Lutheran, the latter two being dominated by the Germans in the village. The Lutheran church had over a thousand congregants, and the Calvinist church several hundred. Everyone usually stayed with their own kind, meaning everyone in the church knew almost everyone else in the church.

And so it happened that Sophie-Néni's brother, Hagel Samuel, and his son, Konrad, appeared at the Schuhmacher door, offering to fix the pigpen for them. Hagel Samuel, whose first wife had died not long before

Christmas after falling through the ice that covered the Marosch River, had recently married a war widow, Kaiser Theresia. The Hagel household had several daughters and had lost two sons to the war. Konrad was the only son left now.

As Elisabeth looked at Konrad, she remembered her conversation with Mammi and Omama. *It's time we start finding you a husband*, Mammi had said. Judging by the giddy looks on her siblings' faces, Elisabeth wondered if they had overheard the conversation yesterday.

Konrad had almost-black hair and deep, brown eyes. He was like any other boy: he hung out with his group of friends and was teased by the older boys when he was young, teased the younger boys when he was older, and eventually had begun learning his father's trade: carpentry. Elisabeth knew that marrying a carpenter, or even a wainwright, would ultimately mean less work for her. On the other hand, because Konrad was the only son in the family now, marrying him would mean moving in with his parents after the ceremony. However, that also meant they would inherit the home when her in-laws passed away. As she weighed her options with Konrad, she decided he was certainly worth getting to know more.

"Welcome, Herr Hagel," Elisabeth said, "and Konrad. Please, come in." She smiled at them gently, in part because she believed Jesus would want it, and in part because

Omama was sitting in the front room with the rest of the family and couldn't see her face.

The father and son removed their hats and stamped the snow off their boots. Elisabeth offered them rags to dry them.

"Thank you," Herr Hagel replied. Konrad also thanked her and smiled at Elisabeth, leaving her with a good first impression. Both men followed Elisabeth in to the front room where everyone else was sitting. The table was decked out in a linen tablecloth Elisabeth had woven a couple of years before, covered by a crocheted runner that had been passed down through Mammi's family. Elisabeth had baked cookies earlier that day—Mammi and Omama had agreed today's visit was a good reason to do so—and they were arranged decoratively on a silver platter, while hot tea steeped in the porcelain teapot. Although the butter cookies were simple circles, Elisabeth had iced them with exquisite floral designs.

"Thank you for coming," Mammi said as the cookies and tea were passed around. "Without my husband here, and with no older boys, managing some of the duties around the house has become hard."

Herr Hagel took a sip of tea. "We're happy to help. Anything you need done, Frau Schuhmacher, please just let us know. Women shouldn't have to take on their husband's work. If you can make some of your goulash while we're here, that will be more than enough payment."

Mammi looked at Elisabeth when she answered. "Because I now look after my husband's shoemaking business, Elisabeth is in charge of the household. It'll be her goulash you'll be tasting."

Konrad made eye contact with Elisabeth, and she smiled back. She offered him the platter of cookies, and he put several on his plate.

"I'll fix your pigpen for you," he said, raising his chest a little.

"Thank you." Elisabeth took a sip of her tea and watched as Konrad threw a cookie into his mouth without so much as noticing her work. "I made the cookies, too," she added.

"They're tasty," Konrad replied, and threw another one into his mouth. His mouth full, he asked, "Have you heard from your father?"

Elisabeth nodded. "He had to find work in a cigar factory, but he said the job is good."

Konrad swallowed. "That must be terrible, being cooped up inside all day like that. No sunlight, no fresh air."

Elisabeth's spirits dropped. She hadn't thought of that. Tata had written about the smell of cigars, but nothing about the work conditions otherwise. No matter the weather, Tata always left the door to his small workshop open to let in fresh air. During harvest season, he helped outside like almost everyone else, and he would get out of his workshop during the day to join the family for meals. Even when Elisabeth's own days were filled, she still had opportunity to go outside. The warmth of the sun on her face would almost feel as though Jesus were talking to her, while the cold chill of the wind helped her focus again on her duties.

"He's doing it to help his family," Elisabeth said.

"Something all men should do," Konrad replied.

Elisabeth took another sip of her tea. "It's something I appreciate."

Konrad smiled at her.

Anna snickered.

Luki kicked Elisabeth's leg.

Rosina ate a cookie as her eyes darted questioningly between her sister and Konrad.

Ignoring her siblings, Elisabeth smiled back.

THE BLOWING SNOW OUTSIDE THAT EVENING MADE ELISABETH shiver, even though she and her family were sitting inside, sharing the warmth that came from the back side of the stove in the front room.

"No, Anna. Pull out the thread and do that stitch again. It's uneven," Omama said. Anna slouched as she unthreaded her needle and pulled the stitch from her embroidery. Elisabeth looked on with a twinge of jealousy:

Anna was constantly praised by Herr Blum for her attentiveness in school. All the adults she encountered remarked at how obedient she was and gently laughed at the simple logic with which she sometimes answered questions. But if Elisabeth asked her to do something and no adults were around, there was a good chance Anna would defy her.

"Let me try!" Rosina insisted as she pulled her knitting back from Elisabeth's hands. Unlike Anna, Rosina didn't pay attention to who was in the room: if she didn't like something or wanted something that she was refused, she said so, and loudly.

Ignoring Omama's warning look, Elisabeth answered her sister, "I'm only trying to help. If you insist on doing it yourself, then fine, but it'll take you longer."

"I want to do it myself!"

Elisabeth shook her head in surrender.

"Rosina," Omama said in a warning tone.

"Please," Rosina replied, and Omama nodded in approval.

"Elisabeth, they will not respect you if you allow that kind of talk," Omama said.

Aware of Mammi's watchful gaze, Elisabeth had to think quickly of what to say. She disagreed with Omama, but she did not want to insult her either.

"I guess I'm too tired this evening," Elisabeth replied, and watched both Omama's and Mammi's faces turn upside down.

"A wife works from the moment she opens her eyes in the morning to the moment she closes them at night," Omama said. "Without a strong wife, a family is nothing. Just look at what my son's family has become." Thankfully, Anna had done something that now impressed Omama, for Omama returned her attention to her. "Yes, beautiful, Anna. Do another stitch just like that one." Anna flicked Elisabeth a smug smile and Elisabeth rolled her eyes. Mammi returned to her knitting, seemingly oblivious to the exchange.

With everyone occupied—Luki was sitting near the stove, using a rubber ball to knock down a group of dried corn cobs that had been cut in half—Elisabeth retrieved a few sheets of paper and a pencil to write a letter to Tata. The straw of her mattress crunched as she sat on her bed, away from the prying eyes of her family. Although the light from the lanterns on the table was thin, she could see enough to write.

February 18, 1920

Dear Tata,

Omama is staying with us. She says it's because Peter-Bátschi's family doesn't show her any respect.

I have been having problems with the others: Herr Blum is ill this week, so school is closed. Monday was horrible. They wouldn't listen to me. I think the only reason they listen to me sometimes now is because of Omama. She spanked

Luki, and since then, I've had fewer problems with the others whenever she is around.

All of us, except Mammi, had the flu a few weeks ago. God took several children to Him through it, but He let us live this time. We also recently learned that two POWs returned from Russia. The war has been over for more than a year now. How many more POWs can there still be?

Cousin Susi is married, so Margarethe-Néni and Konrad-Bátschi now live at home with only Georg and Eva.

Some boards in the animal stalls have begun to splinter and loosen. Omama told Mammi to ask Hagel Samuel and his son, Konrad, to help. Omama and Mammi want to start finding me a husband—they said so! I'm excited and scared. Scared, because I don't know what my future will be. Excited because I will be able to start my own family and also because the earlier I marry, the sooner you will come home.

I have a question to ask you, Tata, but I'm scared of the answer. You wrote about how bad the smell in the cigar factory is, but Hagel Konrad said you also don't have any fresh air or sunlight. Is that true? Does that mean your work days are very hard? If they are, then I will pray even harder to Jesus that your job becomes easier for you.

I have only drawn a few pictures in the sketchbook you bought me: I am so busy here that I hardly have time to draw at all. But I am trying to find time to at least draw the most important things in it.

I miss you, and I hope you stay safe.

Love,

Your Golden One

Elisabeth reread her letter and, satisfied with it, folded it up. Luki's little ball rolled across the floor to her. As she bent over to pick it up, the letter dropped out of her lap. Luki snatched it up.

"Give that back!" Elisabeth said.

"What does it say?" He unfolded it and cocked his head to the side as he tried to decipher the words. "I can't read it."

"If you would pay more attention in class and to me, you might be able to. Now, give it back."

"No!"

Dismayed, Elisabeth stood up and Luki shot into the kitchen.

"Luki!" Omama shouted and banged the table. "Return that letter to your sister at once!"

Luki froze and turned around, fear in his eyes.

"At once, I said," Omama repeated, her voice stern. As Luki walked slowly back to the front room, Omama said to Elisabeth, "*That* is why you spank them."

Elisabeth sighed. She almost wished Luki hadn't listened to their grandmother.

CHAPTER SEVEN

It was Friday morning, the last day of her first week at Eby Heights, and Juliana couldn't be happier. It was first period, enough to make any student complain, but she had figured out a way to schedule her studying for the next couple of weeks so she could cover everything she needed to learn. She had to admit that Jasmine was right again: once she stopped focusing on everything going wrong, Juliana could move ahead in her plans. Unfortunately, it meant she couldn't spend as much time practicing, but for now she didn't have a choice. Competition season didn't start until late February for her new studio, so Juliana would have lots of time to practice afterwards. She just needed to get through this month.

Ms. Haseltine asked everyone to partner up, leaving Juliana in the awkward position of having to wait for someone to choose her. She soon realized that the class had an odd number of students, leaving her with no partner at all. To her relief, the girl beside her, whose name Juliana had finally learned, invited her to join in.

"It's gotta suck not knowing anyone," Meghan said.

"Yeah, pretty much," Juliana replied.

"This is Shawna." Meghan indicated a girl with brown hair and green eyes sitting next to her.

"Hi," Juliana said, happy to finally *meet* people. Shawna looked at her without speaking.

Meghan flipped her pencil through her fingers. "Don't worry about her. She's just quiet."

Ms. Haseltine assigned each group a subject in health studies and asked them to create a list of questions that could be on the exam.

A boy in the next group scoffed. "She probably wants us to come up with the questions for her."

"No, Bradley," the teacher said. "The exam's already been written. I want you to put yourselves in my shoes and figure out the questions. We'll compile a list at the end of class and then you'll all have something to study from."

Another student objected to the exercise and Juliana became impatient. She just wanted to start working: her study schedule had very little wiggle room if she was going to cover everything, and every minute she could use in class was one minute extra at home she could devote to reviewing something else. If her group actually finished their questions early, she could even begin answering the ones she knew the answers to.

Juliana's group was asked to prepare questions on social factors for substance abuse. Juliana opened her binder, which was filled with handouts Ms. Haseltine had given her earlier in the week, and began searching for the topic.

"I'm going to go sharpen my pencil," Meghan said and got up.

"Um, where should we start?" Juliana asked Shawna.

"Doesn't matter," Shawna replied as she began to write down one question after another.

"Do you have this material already memorized?" Juliana asked.

Shawna's only response was a shrug, but as Juliana watched Shawna, she got her answer: yes. By the time Meghan returned, Shawna had already written down five questions. Meghan didn't give Shawna's work a glance, but instead sat down, licked the tip of her pencil, and opened her binder, only to have a chunk of papers slide out and onto the floor.

Juliana was helping Meghan pick up the papers when an idea came to her out of nowhere. "War," she said. "War could be a factor in substance abuse."

"That's not in the material," Shawna said matter-of-factly.

"It's still a social situation. I think, anyway. Just think of what someone sees if they go to war: dead people, people being killed. It can't be easy to come back."

"No different than watching TV," Meghan said.

"No, I think it's pretty different. You can shut off the TV and get back to your normal life. Soldiers can't turn off the war." Juliana raised her hand and asked Ms. Haseltine if war was a possible social cause for substance abuse.

"You know what? I'd really never thought of that before. What made you think of it?"

"I don't know." Juliana paused for a moment. "I guess my grandfather. He told me about a cousin of his who fought in World War I and had what I think would now be called PTSD. I don't know if he drank or took drugs or anything, but apparently everyone made fun of him. That makes it a social situation, doesn't it? I can see it being a problem when thousands of soldiers come back from war and can't cope."

"That's great thinking," Ms. Haseltine said, "but because we didn't cover it in class, it may not help you with the exam."

Juliana felt dejected. She finally thought she knew something. However, Ms. Haseltine had said "may not..." not wouldn't.

Ms. Haseltine walked over to another pair to answer their question.

"War should be an answer," Juliana said.

"I also think I should be the one to win the OFSSA one-hundred-metre swim," Meghan said, "but I won't if I don't do exactly as my coach tells me to."

She had a point. "What questions do you suggest?" Juliana asked.

By now, Shawna had at least fifteen written down, but she didn't look inclined to share them with the group.

"How do friends make you take drugs or drink?" Meghan offered.

"Sounds good."

"Where are you from again?" Meghan asked as they wrote it down.

"Calgary."

Meghan looked up, excited. "Oooh...I'd love to live out there. Those mountains are so awesome. My dream is to swim in a glacier lake at some point."

"Those are cold, you know."

"Yeah, but that's the cool part, no pun intended. I've always imagined that swimming in that clear mountain water has got to be the most amazing experience."

"Meghan," Ms. Haseltine called. "Focus, please."

"Okay," Juliana said. "How about...What do you do when your friend is drunk?"

Meghan and Juliana both wrote it down.

"So what was it like moving here?" Meghan asked.

"Honestly, it's kind of depressing. It's so flat, and there are so many trees, you can't see the horizon. And it's so brown and gray."

"Yeah—we got our snow in November, Christmas had a dusting, then that snowstorm a few days later, and now this. That's normal for us, though this year seems to be a bit on the no-snow extreme side so far."

"But it's less shovelling," Shawna said out of the blue, not taking her eyes off her work.

"Well, we don't have to always shovel tons of snow in Calgary, but when the snow falls, it stays. I can't adjust to this snow-and-thaw thing," Juliana said.

Shawna didn't respond.

"My parents have a snow removal service," Meghan said. "So I wouldn't know."

"Girls," Ms. Haseltine said. "I know it's exciting to have a new class member but you need to get your questions written down."

"Lunch?" Meghan asked.

"Sure." Juliana smiled. Finally!

JULIANA WAS SITTING IN HER BEDROOM, ANSWERING THE questions from health class when she heard the side door to the house open. Her heart skipped a beat as she bolted out of her room to see Dad come into the kitchen. She gave him a huge hug.

"Whoa!" Dad said and chuckled. "Exactly what I was hoping for. I missed you, too."

When Juliana finally let go, he took off his coat and put it in the hallway closet.

"I finally met some girls in school today!"

Dad grinned. "See? I told you that you would. Tell me about them." He put two slices of bread into the toaster and pulled out the peanut butter and strawberry jam.

"Well, one girl's Meghan. She's really nice, but she talks a lot. Our phys ed teacher had to keep telling us to stop talking."

"I hope you listened?"

Juliana looked at the ground. "Well, sort of. I tried."

"Juliana, you need to listen to your teachers."

"I know, I know, but I've spent all week by myself."

The toast popped out of the toaster and Dad put it on his plate.

"Anyways," Juliana continued. "I met one of her friends. Shawna was in phys ed class with us. She's really quiet."

"So she listened to the teacher?" Dad scraped the peanut butter along the toast with his knife.

"Dad, seriously! You told me to tell you about my day."

"I'm also your parent and need to make sure I tell you how to behave in school."

"Can I just talk? Or are you going to constantly interrupt me?"

Dad raised his hands in a fake surrender. "Keep going." He spread the jam on his toast and carried his plate to the table.

"Well, actually, that was it. I mean, I actually ate lunch with someone today, well, two people, so that was pretty cool. And I'm catching up on French pretty easily."

"Good to hear. Keep studying." Dad swallowed a bite of toast. "And how's Opa doing?"

Juliana tucked a piece of hair behind her ear. "I don't know. I thought he was having problems this week, but then he looked like he wasn't. I can't figure out if he's okay or not." She told him about the shirt incident and the apple core.

Dad swallowed again and looked at her, his face serious. "Listen, Jules. If and when things become serious with your Opa, we'll get help. Your mom and her siblings are setting money aside for that. But right now, he's only in the early stages of dementia. There will be blips."

"Okay," she said, somewhat hesitantly. "But one time he said some German words in the middle of his English ones. Is that normal? I couldn't find anything online about that being part of dementia."

Dad smiled. "He's been doing that since I met him. I'm surprised he's actually been able to keep both languages separate until now."

"So you think he's okay?"

Dad nodded. "Things will come and go with him. If you're ever really scared, you can call Mom, me, Aunt Anne, or even Uncle Peter. If he's in town, I'm sure he'll be able to help."

Dad and Juliana talked for a few more minutes, and then Dad lay down for a short nap.

Juliana went to her room to study. She sat at her desk, trying to answer the questions from health class, but after fifteen minutes, she gave up: she couldn't concentrate. When she was first moving in, she was worried Opa would do embarrassing things like drool or eat with his mouth wide open...things she'd heard that old people did. But that hadn't been the case, and the more she tried to figure things out for herself, the more she had begun to worry about him. She opened up the dementia website she had visited the other day and kept reading.

She read about symptoms of dementia in the advanced stages: wandering, emotional outbursts, anger. *Sometimes I wish I couldn't read*, she thought. Would she be able to tell the difference between a normal expression of anger and one caused by his dementia? She hated it when people assumed her behaviour stemmed from her being "just a teen," and so she tried really hard to not see Opa as "just an old man with dementia." But the more she read, the more she realized that dementia could become really serious. How would she know when he had crossed over from these early stages to the more advanced ones? As she read, she learned that dementia could take years to fully develop. But what if Opa was farther along than everyone actually thought? Hadn't Dad suspected that just last week?

She pulled out the book of drawings from her great-grandmother and passed her hand over the stiff, brown leather. How was she going to learn what all these drawings meant before Opa's memory faded forever? In the few weeks she had been living with him, she'd learned from him that his mother had grown up in a house without electricity or a phone, and that it had had a dirt floor. She had taken tours of pioneer homes back in Calgary, and even they had floor boards. No electricity, of course, but at least they weren't walking on dirt, and those homes had been built easily fifty years before the one drawn in this book, maybe even a hundred.

Juliana turned page after page, glancing at each pencil sketch as she went, realizing how little they meant to her. She then paged backwards and eventually stopped at the image of the envelope being opened. Why had it been so special to her great-grandmother? Was she just happy they had mail at all, since they didn't have a telephone? Or had the letter said something important?

She closed her study notes, calculated how much study time she'd lost, and wrote it down so she could try to reschedule it. She then headed downstairs to the basement. If she couldn't concentrate, she might as well get a few questions answered. She knocked on Opa's bedroom door.

"*Ja?*" Opa said.

"Can I come in?" Juliana asked.

"Of course!"

Juliana opened the door and entered. She had only

been inside her grandfather's bedroom once before—to get a better look at her great-grandmother's book after she had discovered it—and at that time it had been clean. This time, though, his clothes were all over his bed, the floor, his night table, and chair. "It's easier to find clothes when they're out here," Opa explained when he saw her look.

She held up her great-grandmother's book. "Can I ask you about this?"

Opa looked confused for a moment, as though he didn't recognize it.

"It's your mom's book of drawings," Juliana said.

Opa's eyes lit up. "Of course! I couldn't quite tell without my glasses." He found his glasses on top of the clothing on his night table and set them on his nose. He pushed aside some of the piles on his bed and made room for Juliana. She sat down beside him and opened the book up to the drawing of a hand opening an envelope.

"I'm trying to figure out why Omama would put this in here. Do you have any idea what's so important about an envelope?"

Opa scratched his balding head as he studied the image. He flipped a few pages ahead and then all the way to the front.

"That's the kitchen...I don't remember what those mittens are about...that's Susi's wedding..." He lost himself in thought for a few moments. "I don't remember when Susi got married. But the envelope...Mammi's father worked in America for some time, so I wonder if this envelope is about something either he wrote or she wrote."

"Were her parents divorced?"

Opa laughed. "No, Yulika, no one divorced back then. You would've shamed your family if you had. He moved to Pennsylvania for..." Opa thought for a moment. "I don't remember how long."

"But didn't you know him?"

Opa shook his head. "He died before I was born. But she loved him and told me about him all the time. No, I think this envelope is about writing to him."

The phone upstairs rang. It was an old phone with a shrill, clanging sound that could be heard throughout the entire house. Opa jumped up to answer it without a word. Was this his dementia or the same eagerness she felt when Rachel texted her?

Still not wanting to study, she walked into the rec room, sat on the thick carpet, and began to stretch. She was still in her day clothes, but she made do and settled into a deep lunge. She couldn't help but wonder what it must have felt like to have a father living all the way across the world and only have letters to communicate with. Maybe Dad's travel wasn't so bad after all.

CHAPTER EIGHT

uki was sitting at the table in the front room, polishing a pair of shoes Mammi had finished. Mammi had again sent Luki inside, which puzzled Elisabeth, because their mother didn't like shoe-making messing up the house. *She's spending a lot of time alone,* Elisabeth thought. *Perhaps she's still sad about Tata.* Whatever the reason, Luki was at least occupied for the time being. In fact, all of Elisabeth's family, save for Mammi, was quietly occupied with one activity or another in the front room: Rosina with her knitting, Anna with her embroidery, and Omama with exquisite crocheting. As fearsome as Omama was, Elisabeth had to admit that the forced quiet she brought with her was a nice blessing. At the very least, it allowed Elisabeth to start working on a pot of goulash for lunch instead of wasting time yelling at her sisters.

Konrad entered the house, letting in a blast of cold air. He and his father had been outside for several hours already, inspecting and repairing the pen. He rubbed his hands together, smiling at Elisabeth as he did so. She smiled back.

"It's nice to have a minute to warm up," he said. "It turns out you have a lot of weakened boards out there."

"Oh? Well, thank you for taking the time to look."

"Of course. We'll get them all fixed for you, and properly."

"If we need to pay for supplies, please let me know."

Konrad nodded. "Where's Luki? I came in to get him: we have some tasks he can help us with."

Elisabeth pointed in the front room. "He's polishing some shoes for Mammi. Luki? It's time to set those down and go out and help Konrad and Herr Hagel."

"I'm not done," Luki said.

Please, Luki, not in front of Konrad and Omama, Elisabeth thought. "I can finish those up for you. It's time for you to go outside and help."

"Luki," Omama said, a threatening tone in her voice. "You are the man of the house. You must help those who have come to help you."

Luki paused for a moment as his gaze moved from Omama to Elisabeth to Konrad, giving Elisabeth hope that he might stop his fight before it got worse. She even prayed to Jesus for a bit of extra help.

"No," Luki said with the confidence of a grown man. "It's cold outside."

Elisabeth shot an apologetic look to Konrad, wiped her hands on her apron, and walked into the front room. Jesus must have been busy with another family right now or He was angry at Elisabeth for something. She would have to settle this on her own.

"Luki, now. Please."

"No!"

Between clenched teeth, Elisabeth said, "You're embarrassing your family. Stop this *now*."

Almost tauntingly, Luki glared at Elisabeth. "I'm *not* going outside."

Omama stood up. "This is enough," she declared. "Luki, either you go with Konrad and help, or you can kneel in the box of corn."

Jesus, what do I do? Elisabeth prayed. Unfortunately, the answer came from Omama instead.

"Lissika," she said, "you must discipline him."

Elisabeth couldn't do it. There had to be a kinder way of forcing Luki to do what was needed. Her brother certainly wasn't Jesus—Jesus hadn't thrown tantrums when He was a child—but he was human, like Jesus. Making Luki kneel in corn seemed almost as painful as placing a crown of thorns on Jesus' head.

Konrad stayed where he was, by the front door, and watched the entire event in silence.

"Luki," Elisabeth said, "you'll be a man someday. You have to learn this."

"No!"

Elisabeth looked up at everyone. She saw nothing but disapproval from Omama. Anna and Rosina, though, looked worried.

"It's cold outside!" Luki protested. "I'm not going! It's not fair that everyone else gets to stay inside."

"That is it," Omama declared. She hobbled as fast as she could into the kitchen, pulled out the box of dried corn kernels, and carried it into the front room. "Luki, roll up your pants!" she commanded.

"No!"

Omama's face turned so angry, Elisabeth almost wondered if the Devil had gotten hold of her. Omama hobbled back to Luki and grabbed him by the ear. His shouts of protest now turned into cries of pain. Elisabeth didn't know what to do: she wanted to protect her brother, but she knew she had to listen to her grandmother or she would be next in line after him and their family would become the gossip of the congregation alongside Peter-Bátschi's family.

Jesus, why can't You help me? she prayed silently.

"Roll up your pants!" Omama repeated.

An idea came to Elisabeth. "Omama, please, let me,"

she said. Omama looked doubtful. "I know what to do," Elisabeth insisted. Omama let go.

Luki tried to dart away, but Elisabeth grabbed him by the arm. "Stay here." Luki tried to pull free of his sister's grip, but Elisabeth held tight. "When I let go of you, go get your coat on. I know how to keep you warm."

Luki's normally sweet face had by now turned ugly with defiance, but before he could say another word, Elisabeth explained. "I promise. You must help outside, but I can make it a little easier for you. Now, get your mittens on, the black ones that Mammi made especially for you for Christmas, and get on your coat."

Elisabeth let go but prepared herself in case Luki attempted to escape again. To her relief, he didn't move, and Elisabeth sent a silent thank you to Jesus. Maybe He was keeping an eye on her after all.

"When Tata comes home and sees the new pigpen, you'll be able to tell him you helped," Elisabeth said. "Now, go get dressed." He finally listened.

While Luki put on his coat, Elisabeth found rags in the front room, opened the oven, and reached inside with a pair of tongs to pull out a few pieces of coal. She wrapped them up tightly and by the time Luki had emerged from the back room, ready to put on his boots, she had little bundles of warmth prepared for him. She placed one in each pant and coat pocket, four in total. "If your fingers get cold, warm them up in your pockets," she instructed.

Elisabeth caught a frown on Konrad's face, which disturbed her. Did he really expect her to send her brother out in the frigid winter without a source of heat for his small, skinny body? It was not the same as when Luki ran about with his friends after school, coming home all sweaty even in the winter. Instead, he would be standing outside by the pigpens, without any sunlight to warm him, and with cold winds blowing around.

A smile appeared on her brother's face and Elisabeth tapped him on the back of his shoulder. "Now, get out there and help Herr Hagel and Konrad with the repairs. I'll even add a little note to my letter to Tata that you helped." At that last suggestion, Luki's chest lifted. "I have to go see the postman in a bit to mail my letter," Elisabeth continued. "When I return, we'll see how you're doing, all right? If Herr Hagel and Konrad approve, you can come inside and do some reading."

Luki's chest fell. "I hate reading," Luki said.

"You need to read for school," Elisabeth said gently.

Omama scowled. "Nonsense," she said. "A man who can maintain his house and farmland is more useful than a man who can read. The Hagels are here now and can teach Luki what a man needs to know. He can read again when he returns to school."

Konrad spoke up. "Father told me not to worry about reading. Luki, one day, you'll marry, and providing for your family will be your purpose. I've barely read a thing since I finished school. Let's work on the pigpens and make your father proud."

Elisabeth was dumbfounded. What she had meant as a way of encouraging Luki to go outside had turned into Konrad discouraging her brother from reading. She didn't know what to say next, but it didn't matter. Konrad put his arm around Luki and ushered him out to the pigpens.

"As it should be," Omama muttered. "Now, everyone, back to work."

How can someone hate reading? Elisabeth thought as she retrieved her letter to add a note about Luki. Her father's encyclopedia, for example, helped her see where he now lived. She knew it was far away, but to see it on a map and read about the country comforted her a little. When Elisabeth had read Tata's letter again to her sisters the other day, hearing Tata's own words had awoken in them their love for him. Today she would mail him her reply. She missed him dearly, but she knew where he was and that he was safe because of his letter. Reading gave Elisabeth almost as much comfort as her faith in Jesus.

How could Konrad hate reading? Elisabeth finished her note in the letter, put it back in its envelope, sealed it shut, and continued preparing her goulash, unable to answer the question.

"Ugh, I don't want to see another book! I can barely think anymore!" Juliana complained as she entered the kitchen that morning, her hands pressing against her head as though she was trying to squeeze juice out of it. Two weeks had passed, and she had one exam behind her, with two more to go. Today was phys ed and health. Tomorrow was French. She had tied her hair up in a loose bun so it wouldn't bother her and had put on her most comfortable leggings and sweater, but despite her morning shower, she felt exhausted and half-asleep, even though she had actually slept eight hours.

"*Guten morgen*," Opa said as he sat at the table eating breakfast.

Juliana ignored him, her nerves forcing her to focus, and she began reciting what she'd studied. "Religion and socio-economic status can affect someone's ability to buy healthy food. Environmental factors that affect healthy food choices include transportation systems, packaging, and...and...food production. Age is also a factor that can affect someone's ability to buy healthy food. What's the best choice to reduce my carbon footprint? Buying local food."

"You'll do fine," Mom said as she handed Juliana a bowl of oatmeal with cut-up apples and a sprinkle of cinnamon.

"What?" Opa asked.

"It can be hard to ship healthy food to the far north of Ontario. Someone might be interested in learning about traditional foods their ancestors ate."

"Nothing, Tata," Mom said over Juliana's recitations. "She's just reviewing her material. It means she's stressed and she needs to be left alone. She started this in grade six out of nowhere. It's not going to make any sense to you, but it's how she calms herself."

"Oh!" Opa held a finger to his lips, indicating that he would stop talking.

Juliana continued reciting one fact after another for her exam, and when she had food in her mouth, she recited the facts silently in her head. She hated studying, but if she was going to maintain her ninety percent average, she had to do it.

"I should be home in time to cook tonight," Mom said, and Juliana nodded in acknowledgement.

"Mental health issues can cause someone to withdraw from relationships."

"Dad texted me to wish you luck on your exam today. He didn't want to risk disturbing your studies by sending you a message."

"Talking about suicide may be a call for help."

"What?" Opa asked, visibly alarmed. "This is what they learn in school?"

"Tata, not now," Mom said to him. Then to Juliana, "You'll do fine. Just this one and French tomorrow, and then you're free for the rest of the week!" Mom grabbed her keys and headed out. "Good luck!" she said as she closed the door behind her.

"Good friends help their friends get help. Help can include community elders, therapists...crap. What else?"

"Family?" Opa offered.

"Yes! Family! And community health service providers, telephone help lines..."

Opa carried his bowl to the sink. "I have a doctor's appointment today," he said, interrupting Juliana's list. "But I'll be home before you get here. Annie is driving me."

"Okay," she said, only half-registering what Opa had said. "When do you call 911? Life-threatening emergencies. What are examples of life-threatening emergencies? Heart attack, choking, stroke—"

"And make sure you put on warm clothes today, Yulika. The windchill out there is -25 or something like that."

Opa's statement derailed Juliana's chaotic train of thought. "What?"

"They said it's going to get really cold. So put on warm clothes."

Juliana stared down at her thin leggings and sweater. The temperatures had dipped back down to below zero, and there was snow on the ground again, but she didn't know it would get *that* cold that fast. "Okay, I'll figure it out." Then her train of thought got back on track. "When do else do you call 911? Frostbite, heat stroke—"

"I'm going to shower."

"Stop interrupting me," Juliana said as she continued to spit out first-aid facts.

"Yulika, you will do fine," Opa said. "Have a good day. I'll see you later. Good luck!"

Juliana nodded. "When else do you call 911? Broken leg, sprained ankle, dislocated hip, slipping..." A sudden fear overcame Juliana: what if Opa fell in the shower and he broke his leg or split his head open? There'd be no one here to help him. She ran to the top of the stairs. "Opa, why don't you wait until someone's home? You know, just to make sure you're safe?"

Disappointment flashed across Opa's face. "Don't tell me you're thinking like that, too," he said.

That wasn't a reaction she had anticipated. "Oh, no, Opa, it's just that, well..." Juliana didn't know what to say.

"I'm fine. I forget a few things now and then, but I can

shower by myself. I'm not stupid," he said and stomped down the stairs.

Juliana froze. She hadn't meant to insult him. But if he did slip on the wet floor, there'd be no one home to help him, and he didn't even have a cordless phone in the house to take with him should he need to call for help. Should she run after him to ask him to wait again? Or should she apologize?

One look at the clock told her she had to boot it to school. She needed to be there at least thirty minutes beforehand so she could start reciting facts there in the hopes of making use of the environment to help her remember things during the exam. It was a tip she'd read online.

"Opa, I'm really sorry!" she shouted downstairs one last time before grabbing her things and running out the door.

JULIANA WATCHED THE CLOCK ON THE CLASSROOM WALL ticking away, each second gone once the second hand had passed it. *And that's one more second you've missed and will never get back*, she thought as she returned her attention to her exam. The next question read "Explain a social situation where you might be pressured to drink. How would you get out of it?"

Juliana described being at a party where people were

drinking. After a few minutes of writing, she re-read her answer. Satisfied with it, she moved on to the next question: "List five situations in which you might call 911 and then write down what you would say to the operator."

Ha! I know this! she thought, but before she could command her hand to start writing, she remembered her worries about Opa. Was he okay? What if he had fallen in the shower? The second hand kept ticking away and she made herself begin writing.

1. Heart attack. Address, the person's age, sex, name if known, not breathing, suspected heart attack.

Then Juliana remembered that Aunt Anne was picking up Opa, and she immediately felt relieved.

2. Heat stroke. Address, age, sex, name. Breathing pattern, flushed.

But what if Aunt Anne had found Opa on the floor and now they were at the hospital? No, that would be okay, right? He was at least getting care. But what if he'd died and Juliana could've prevented it by calling someone?

Get a grip! she admonished herself. *It's just dementia! He's fine!* She wrote down, *3. Drowning.*

But I really didn't mean to make him angry, she thought. *I hope I didn't ruin his day or something. Will he tell Mom?*

She paged through the entire exam and then looked up at the clock. She still had fifty-five minutes, and there was one short essay question at the end she had to budget time for.

You can do this, she thought to herself, but then her mind drifted again to Opa.

JULIANA DRAGGED HERSELF INTO THE HOUSE AFTER HER EXAM.

"Hi," Opa said cheerfully from the kitchen table. He was dressed neatly in a turtleneck with a knitted vest over it, reminding Juliana of ads for retirement homes and dentures. "How was your exam?"

"I think I aced it," she said. At his confused look, she explained, "I did really well."

"That's wonderful!"

Juliana remembered Opa's appointment and asked him about it, but Opa waved his hand, dismissing the question. "Nothing important," he said.

His reaction puzzled her. The other day, he had been thrilled because his pee was fine, but now he wasn't happy. Juliana guessed that something had happened. Given how he'd reacted this morning, though, she wasn't sure if she should ask him. "Well, if you want to talk about it..."

"No, I'm fine," he said. "There's nothing wrong with me and I wish everyone would stop acting like there was. I can look after myself, and I certainly don't need your family here to babysit me."

Juliana stood still. What was she supposed to say to that?

Opa took a stack of neatly folded tea towels from under the sink and walked to the stairs.

"What do you need those for?" Juliana asked. "Did something spill?"

Opa's mood changed again, and he said in a tone that suggested the answer was obvious, "They're dirty and they need cleaning. I can look after myself, Yulika."

He disappeared into the basement and Juliana stared after him. There was no need for him to wash those tea towels.

"*Verdammt nochamol!*" she heard from downstairs.

Part of Juliana wanted to rush downstairs and see if he needed help, but part of her was scared he would get angry at her again. She continued to listen to hear whether she was needed. A metallic bang startled her, but just as she was about to head down, she heard Opa grumbling to himself as he shuffled to his room and closed the door behind him. She could hear that he had turned on his television so she tiptoed down and into the laundry room. The stack of tea towels was all over the floor. Was he angry because he'd dropped them? She inspected the washing machine to make sure it wasn't damaged and then noticed a more likely cause of Opa's frustration: a small light glowed on the machine, and next to it were the words "child lock."

A child lock for a grown man. That would make Juliana angry, too.

CHAPTER TEN

"Let's go!" Elisabeth urged her sisters as she pushed the pot of goulash into the oven. The mailman only showed up once a week to take mail and deliver the week's news, and she finally had an opportunity to listen to what he had to say. She waited impatiently by the house door as her sisters finished tying their boots.

"Hurry!" she said. "I don't want to miss the news!"

"But I want to stay home," Rosina pouted.

Elisabeth bent down to Rosina's height and whispered, "And stay alone with Omama?"

Rosina's mood changed in the blink of an eye. Anna must have heard, too, for she also stepped up her pace. Elisabeth tiptoed into the back room, where Omama was snoring soundly, to get their shawls, headscarves, and mittens. Each girl dressed herself, and Elisabeth pulled her dress sleeves down extra hard: she hated it when cold air travelled up them.

The sky was gray, and outside, the temperature must have been around minus ten Celsius. Each girl had several shawls pulled tightly around her, and all three scurried along the side of the house to the front gate and out into the street, when Elisabeth suddenly stopped.

"What are we waiting for?" Anna asked.

"*Shh...*"

Her sisters stared at her, puzzled, but then she heard it: a laugh from Luki. It meant that, for now, he was listening and hopefully eagerly helping the Hagels. Satisfied, Elisabeth led her sisters to the town hall, which lay about three blocks west of their home.

"Were you listening for Konrad?" Anna asked, a mischievous smile on her face.

Elisabeth shook her head.

"Are you going to marry him?" Rosina asked.

"It's too early to tell," Elisabeth said.

"But he likes you," Anna followed up. "I can tell."

"Oh, really?" Elisabeth asked. "And just what did you see?"

"He smiled at you." Anna made kissing noises.

"Stop that!" Elisabeth said.

"Would he be a good husband?" Anna continued.

"I think so," Elisabeth said, but no sooner had she

answered Anna's question than she doubted her answer's truthfulness. "He's learning how to be a carpenter from his father, and their family farm uses day-labourers on their land. It means I wouldn't have to work as hard as Mammi does." That did sound like a good match, didn't it?

The postman began drumming in the distance to announce his arrival to anyone nearby. The sound distracted her from any further thoughts on the matter as she picked up her pace even more.

"Like Eva?" Anna asked as she tried to keep up.

"Sort of. She and Georg will have their house passed down to them and they won't have to pay for it. So that makes things easier for them, and that would happen to me, too, if I married Konrad. However, Eva and Georg don't have any day-labourers on their farm like the Hagels do." She then thought about her cousin Georg's shaking episodes and wondered how those would affect his ability to look after his land. "But maybe they will hire help one day," she added.

"Wait for me!" Rosina called from a few steps behind them. Elisabeth turned around, smiled at her youngest sister, and beckoned her to hurry.

"Does Konrad have the shakes like Georg?" Anna asked, worried. Elisabeth thought back to the day when she and Anna had been helping with wedding preparations at their aunt and uncle's house. After seeing Anna's red mittens, Georg had erupted into an inexplicable panic and collapsed in a fit. That episode had troubled Anna greatly.

Elisabeth placed a hand on her sister's shoulder. "No, he doesn't. He didn't fight in the war, and that affliction only affects soldiers. Well, some of them, anyway."

Anna breathed a sigh of relief.

"But if you marry him," Rosina said, "that means you'll move out of our house and in with the Hagels. Tata's already gone. I don't want you to leave."

Elisabeth smiled at her youngest sister. "Rosina, even if I did marry him, it wouldn't be for at least another year: Tata said he would be home before I marry but he also wanted to stay away for a year. Besides, I'd have to get to know Konrad a little better first." She patted Rosina on the back.

The drumming got louder and faster, and Elisabeth hurried, now leaving her sisters behind. She waved at people she knew, including her best friend, Maria, but as much as she longed to stop to talk with them, she needed to make sure she mailed her letter to Tata and heard the week's news. It was the next best thing to listening in on visits from the men in the village.

She arrived to find the usual crowd of people surrounding the postman, who was still drumming away to call attention to anyone near the town hall. As Elisabeth tried to push her way through the crowd to get closer to the front, her sisters ran to catch up, bumping into her before they could stop. She stumbled into a man standing in front of her.

"I'm sorry," she said to him, and before she could scold her sisters, the man turned around. Elisabeth found herself looking up at Georg. Anna immediately hid herself behind Elisabeth and tucked her red-mittened hands under her armpits. Rosina just stared at him. His hulking stature and expressionless face often frightened people, and his sudden outbursts fed the gossip circles weekly, embarrassing not only his wife but his entire family. Many in the village called him "crazy" and "weak." Although Elisabeth had never particularly liked him growing up, in her eyes now he had become a sad ghost: his body was there, but she could tell his mind was often not, as though it was travelling somewhere between Earth and Heaven. She pitied him now. His life was in shambles all because a few people they didn't know had chosen to fight each other and to drag their countries into a conflict that had killed millions, mostly men.

Next to Georg stood one of the two prisoners of war, the POWs she had seen in church and whom Peter-Bátschi had talked about, including the one with the missing arm. Elisabeth's eyes fixated on his stump, making her forget her manners. The man stood at about the same height as Georg, but he was very thin, about a third of the size of Georg's large frame. His brown hair stuck out in different directions from under his cap, suggesting it was a little longer than usual for men in the village. He was definitely older than Elisabeth, but he looked younger than Georg.

"Will it grow back?" Rosina asked in wonder. "His arm?"

"Rosina!" Elisabeth scolded. Her cheeks burned, both because of her own reaction to the missing limb and that of her sister's. But she did notice the corners of Georg's mouth turning up just a little.

The man tipped his hat, a charming smile on his face. "I'm Stefan Schäfer."

Elisabeth came to her senses. "I'm sorry," she said, now flustered.

"It's all right," Stefan said. "It's not a usual sight."

"Oh, no, it's not that!" Elisabeth replied, trying to cover up her behaviour. Of course, it was exactly his missing arm that flustered her so much, but she couldn't say that. That would have been impolite.

"These are my cousins," Georg said, relieving her of any further awkwardness, and introducing each of the sisters by name. "You may have met Lukas-Bátschi when we were younger. The shoemaker?"

"I think so," Stefan said to the sisters. "I'm sorry, I tried so hard to hold on to memories of Semlak, but—"

"They don't need to hear about it," Georg said gently.

Stefan didn't continue with his explanation, but Elisabeth longed to hear it. If anything, it would have opened the door a little more to understanding Georg's mind and maybe could help her assist him somehow. She glanced quickly at Anna and thanked Jesus that her sister still hid her mittens. What if they upset Stefan, too?

Georg continued with the introductions. "Stefan is cousins with Tiny Hay, and he's a friend of mine and Samuel's." Georg was referring to his brother, of course, and not Hagel Samuel.

"Oh, yes?" Elisabeth said. Stefan looked familiar to her, but whether it was because she had known him fleetingly from her childhood or because he looked like someone else, she couldn't tell. Then again, everyone in their congregation looked familiar, because almost everyone followed the same dress code and saw each other every Sunday at church, as well as sometimes Tuesdays or Thursdays during the winter at weddings, and on any day at christenings and funerals and dances.

The postman's drumming stopped. Both men and the three sisters turned to face him as he announced the week's headlines.

"Arad under threat to be left without charcoal!"

"No charcoal in Arad?" someone interrupted.

"None," the postman confirmed. "The central directorship of the Romanian Railway in Cluj has stopped supplying Arad with charcoal as of Tuesday. It proposed that the electrical plant be transformed so that wood can be used instead of charcoal."

"What is the city doing about it in the meantime?" someone else asked.

"Mayor Robu asked that General Leca intervene. The newspapers say that progress was made by appealing to the Transylvanian troop commanders."

A few murmurs travelled through the crowd, but the postman continued.

"Butchers and sausage-makers of Arad ask the price supervisory committee to increase their prices!

"A reminder: the chief physician of the city of Arad asks all practitioners to report to him all cases of the Spanish flu and other cases of contagious diseases!

"Victorious Romania pulls more soldiers out of Budapest!"

Elisabeth didn't like hearing about the Hungarian-Romanian war that had begun immediately after the end of the bigger war that had seemed to pull in the whole world and that had caused so much suffering. It was hard enough to live now in a country that had been her homeland's enemy. Although Tata had said that many of the people who lived in the Banat, the large region Semlak was in, had voted to join Romania, Elisabeth still could not wrap her mind around the simple fact that her home was now part of what she had always thought of as enemy territory. Immediately after that great war had finished, Romania had declared war on Hungary, and although that war had ended last summer, she had heard that Romanian troops continued to occupy Budapest this entire time. She shook her head at the futility of so much war and stared again at Stefan's missing arm.

"Now for your mail," the postman announced, interrupting her thoughts.

"That's a concern about the charcoal, isn't it, Georg?" Stefan said as the postman began handing out packages. "Hopefully the shortage doesn't affect blacksmiths."

Georg, who was a blacksmith, only grunted.

Elisabeth waited in the short line to hand the postman her letter. He inspected the stamp, tipped his hat to her, and tucked the letter inside his bag. By the time she turned around with her siblings to return home, Georg and Stefan were already on their way back to Georg's home. Anna could finally shake out her mittened hands.

"Anna, Rosina, I need to ask for a big promise from both of you," Elisabeth said as they returned home. Elisabeth's sisters looked up at her. "I know you don't like to listen to me, but so long as Omama is staying in our home, can you please do as I say? I promise I won't make you do anything you shouldn't normally do, but if you yell at me, Omama will yell at all of us and may discipline us like she has Luki."

Anna looked suspicious, while Rosina said defiantly, "Then I'll run away from her."

"And do what?" Elisabeth asked. "Sleep out in the stalls with the cows and horses at night? She will catch you at some point. The problem is that I want to look after all of you, but I don't want to embarrass Mammi."

"What do we get in return?" Anna asked.

"Pardon me?" Elisabeth said. "What do you get in return? I'm asking you, my sisters, to help me here. I'd rather you listened to me all the time—Mammi has put me in charge of the household—but all I'm asking is that, so long as Omama is here, you do your best to behave."

They walked a little farther while her sisters seemed to deliberate her request. Before they answered, Rosina squinted her eyes in concentration and asked, "What's that noise?"

The other two stopped and listened.

"Just someone's animals," Elisabeth replied and continued walking. But as they neared their street, "just someone's animals" turned into panicked squealing, clucking, quacking, and honking, and once they turned onto their street, Elisabeth could see pigs on the road in front of their home. She lifted the front of her skirt and began to run.

"Wait for me!" Rosina cried.

"I can't!" Elisabeth yelled back. "I think it's *our* animals!"

When she arrived at the front gate, Elisabeth shrieked:

their pigs had gotten loose, with several on the road and the rest in the front yard, dangerously near the open gate. All the birds were flapping madly about in their coops as they sounded the alarm. Omama was standing underneath the overhang, shaking her fist at the Hagels, and Mammi had an arm wrapped across her waist as she shouted at them.

Luki was nowhere to be seen.

CHAPTER ELEVEN

Juliana practically skipped all the way home, the frigid air stinging her lungs. Today's windchill had apparently hit minus thirty Celsius, and rumour had it that exams had almost been postponed because of it. She still couldn't figure out how people here could live when temperatures could fluctuate by more than thirty degrees in a week, but it didn't matter! She was done! Although she had only had three exams, she had spent so much time studying the material that her brain felt like a plate of ground beef.

"Which can be a good source of iron," she said aloud. "Stop it! You're done!" She came up to a patch of ice and slid across it, shouting, "You're done!" She couldn't wait to begin practicing again: now that she had caught up on her schoolwork, she could focus again on catching up on her dancing.

The energy in her threatened to spill over into a tight bear hug with the first person she saw when she arrived home. At the door, she searched for her keys in her backpack. Her excitement coursing through her entire body, she couldn't keep her fingers still enough to pull her key out in one try. Getting the key into the lock required as much concentration as trying a double pirouette *en pointe*.

The lock finally turned and she threw the door open.

"I'm home and I'm done!" she shouted. She slammed the door behind her out of exuberance, kicked off her boots, and leaped over the two stairs to the kitchen. "Opa! I'm home!" She ran into her bedroom, threw her backpack onto her bed, only to watch it topple and crash onto the floor.

"And you know what?" she said into the air. "I don't care! I'm done! I did it!"

She ran back into the kitchen. "Opa?" she called out again. She paused for a moment to listen for the familiar creaks in the house. After a few seconds of silence, she ran downstairs, panicking that something had happened. She peeked into Opa's room, the rec room, the bathroom, the laundry room, and even the fruit cellar, where she had found Omama's book, but he wasn't there.

She ran back up into the kitchen and was about to call

her aunt when she saw an entry on his calendar: "Deutsch Klub 2:30."

"Oh." Juliana's excitement deflated faster than a balloon. She grabbed her usual snack and water and dropped into a chair at the table. A moment ago she had been brimming with joy, and now sitting in the small, empty house, with no one to welcome her home on the day when she had actually triumphed, that joy churned inside her stomach, transforming into uncomfortable feelings she tried to push away.

"No," she said, "this can't be happening to me. I've made it through this month, and there's no one to tell?" Now anger began to seep in. "How can there be no one here?" Her mother was one of three, her aunt had six kids and lived nearby, Opa was usually home, and despite all that, there was no one else in the house.

She returned to her room, shut the door, and stared at herself in the mirror.

"You're the only one here to celebrate with," she said to herself. "Rachel's in Calgary, and Jasmine, Meghan, and Shawna have their regular friends." Tears began to well up in her eyes. "Dad's in Florida again, Mom's at work, and Opa's with his friends. And you're here alone."

The tears flowed stronger now. Whenever she and her old dance team had won a big award, Miss Kasia had ordered in pizza. And whenever she and Rachel wanted to celebrate anything, whether it was an award at a dance competition, or someone's birthday, or passing a major test at school, they had a sleepover and watched movies all night.

"This isn't fair," she said. "Why am I being left behind?"

Juliana's loneliness weighed on her so much that she didn't even have the heart to dance. She collapsed into her bed and fell asleep.

JULIANA SQUINTED AT THE SUDDEN BRIGHT LIGHT AND SHE heard someone call her name. She shielded her eyes as she sat up and saw Sophie. What was Sophie doing in her bedroom?

"Hey," Juliana said, her voice groggy. "Is everything okay?"

The confused expression on her cousin's face told Juliana she'd asked the wrong question.

"Is everything okay with *you*?" Sophie asked.

Juliana at first nodded and then remembered Sophie might not have seen her reaction: her cousin was losing her sight at the centre of her vision. "Yeah, I'm fine. Why?"

"We were worried," Sophie replied. "We tried calling you, but you didn't answer your phone or the house phone."

Had Juliana really slept that deeply that she hadn't heard the house phone's shrill ring? And how could she not have heard her cell? But one glance at her backpack on the floor suggested her phone had gotten buried in the fall.

"We were going to take you and Opa out for supper instead of cooking tonight," Sophie continued, "but then you didn't pick up."

"Yulika?" Opa called from the hallway.

"She's in her room, Opa," Sophie called back. Juliana heard Opa's familiar steps.

"Are you sure you're okay?" Sophie asked.

"Yeah," Juliana replied, though her voice sounded more like a frog's croak.

She rubbed her eyes and stood up just as Opa entered. He stared at her face for a moment. "Your eyes are puffy. Were you crying?"

Juliana shook her head, but Opa insisted. Just then, another set of footsteps travelled down the hallway and Juliana looked over Opa's shoulder to see Aunt Anne.

"Juliana?"

By now, Juliana was frustrated and embarrassed. When she wanted someone home to celebrate with, there was no one. When she wanted privacy, everyone showed up.

"She's been crying, Anne," Opa said.

And now they're talking about me like I'm not even here, she thought.

"What's wrong?" Aunt Anne asked.

"Nothing," Juliana said, frustration creeping in to replace the tiredness in her voice.

"Tata, Sophie, can you leave us alone for a minute?"

Great. Now I get "a talk," Juliana thought as her cousin and grandfather returned to the kitchen.

"I know we hardly know each other, but I can tell you're upset," Aunt Anne said. Her voice was gentle, but the last thing Juliana wanted to do right now was talk.

"I'm fine, just tired," Juliana replied. She dug her phone out of her bag and glanced at its clock: it was late enough that Rachel might be available now. *Crap—she's at the studio all evening*, she remembered. *Still no one to talk to.* "Really, I'm okay. Just exhausted from the past few weeks."

Aunt Anne studied her. "You had your last exam today, didn't you?"

Juliana nodded.

"And no one was here to celebrate with you."

Juliana could feel her tears returning, and she closed her eyes to try and push them back. Aunt Anne immediately pulled her phone out of her jacket pocket. She tapped it a few times and then held it up to her ear. "I'm trying your mom."

Juliana sighed. If she'd been allowed to just sleep a little longer and then refresh herself—in private—no one would have noticed and she could just move on. Her parents had made it clear to her that they had to work, so what was the point in trying to get a hold of them? As if confirming her thoughts, Aunt Anne shook her head.

"She's not answering. Well, it is student discount night.

Maybe they're swamped. I'll try your dad." Moments later, Aunt Anne shook her head. "Nope, he's not answering either. What did you do after exams back in Calgary?"

"Hung out with Rachel and my other friends usually."

"And you don't know anyone well enough here yet." Aunt Anne tapped her phone a few times and then started texting. "We're going out as planned and we're going to celebrate your last day of exams." She looked up from her phone at Juliana, who knew she had to nod, because anything else would've been rude. Aunt Anne continued tapping on her phone. "I'm just letting your parents know."

"I have dance tonight."

"That's fine. Pack your stuff. If Katy isn't able to get away from work in time, we'll just take you after we finish eating. I'll wait for you in the kitchen."

As Juliana packed her dance bag, she had to admit that she felt a little relieved. She didn't want the attention, but her aunt trying to make her feel better was, well, nice. And once she was at the studio, she'd at least be able to talk to Jasmine.

She'll probably tell me to stop brooding, Juliana thought. But then she realized that maybe that was exactly what she needed right now.

CHAPTER TWELVE

"I told you not to pull down both boards!" Hagel Samuel shouted at his son.

"You did not!" Konrad replied.

"Yes, I did tell you!"

"Well, if Luki hadn't been in the way, I would've done my job right!"

"If you had closed the gates behind you when you came back with those boards, the animals wouldn't be on the road now!"

The father and son argued back and forth, blaming each other and Elisabeth's brother without solving anything while the family's pigs kept roaming freely all over the road and front yard, and the ducks, geese, and chickens made more noise than three bad bands at a wedding. Elisabeth knew she and her sisters had to act quickly but also that the unpredictable animals in the yard were too dangerous for Rosina, so she instructed her youngest sister to go inside and find Luki. Elisabeth immediately closed the gate to keep the remaining pigs from escaping.

"Mammi! Can you help?" Elisabeth called. Mammi shook her head, her hand still over her stomach, which now worried Elisabeth: was Mammi sick? But she had no time to think about that right now.

"Anna, it's up to us," she said. Anna swallowed and clung to Elisabeth. "Stay calm," she said. "I know this looks scary, but if we panic, it will make things worse, understand?" Anna nodded, though she didn't show any signs of calming down. "Keep an eye on the pigs on the road and yell to me if they run. I'll be back shortly with corn," Elisabeth reassured her. Anna nodded again and then turned around to perform her duty. For now, the pigs on the road seemed calm, happy to roam and search for food, and Elisabeth hoped they would stay that way.

Elisabeth walked through the front yard as calmly as she could, doing her best to avoid the running pigs, and entered the poultry yard. The Hagels were still yelling at each other, ignoring the agitated animals.

"Herr Hagel," she said, "please repair the pigpen."

"My son must fix his mistake!" he insisted and continued arguing with Konrad.

Elisabeth shook her head in disbelief as she tried to think of what to say next.

"Elisabeth!" Anna yelled. But it was not the pigs Elisabeth saw when she turned around. Instead she saw Georg and Stefan standing outside the front yard and Anna tucking her mittened hands into her armpits again.

"Do you need help?" shouted Stefan. Georg remained still but waiting. With their family home not too far away, they must have heard the noise. Elisabeth smiled when she saw Anna urgently nod in answer to the question. Elisabeth beckoned for them to enter.

She turned back to face Konrad's father. "If we're to get the pigs back into their pen, we need those boards up immediately, Herr Hagel. It doesn't matter who's at fault: all that matters in Jesus' eyes is that we help each other. So please, both of you, just repair it."

The Hagels looked stunned, and Elisabeth could tell by the look on Konrad's face that he did not approve of Elisabeth telling him what to do. But Elisabeth could not care less: the pigs had escaped their pen and the birds flapped and squawked frantically. If the yard was not brought back to order, the animals could begin hurting each other. Elisabeth implored the Hagels one more time, and only then did they return to the pigpen to finish the repair.

Stefan and Georg by now had reached Elisabeth.

"Let's get the birds calmed first," Stefan said. "That noise sounds worse than a volley of gunshots." He covered one ear with his hand, but his stump also lifted, as though he still had his other hand with which he could cover his other ear.

Doing her best to ignore the odd sight, Elisabeth shook her head. "We need the animals brought back into the poultry yard first. Then we calm the birds down while the Hagels finish the repair," she said above the oinking, quacking, and squawking.

"One pig's wandering away!" Anna yelled at the top of her lungs from the road. Elisabeth signalled that she had heard.

Georg turned to Stefan. "This is Elisabeth's house. We should do as she wishes," he said, surprising Elisabeth. Stefan nodded and Elisabeth proceeded to direct them.

The two men headed for the wagon shed and each retrieved a sheet of wood to herd the animals off the road. Elisabeth grabbed a pail that hung outside the chicken coop and filled it with cobs of corn from the *hambar*. When she dropped several cobs on the ground in the front yard, the pigs there calmed down at the sight of easy-to-reach food.

Anna pulled her hand out of her mitten and opened the gate for Georg, Stefan, and Elisabeth. Step by step, the two men used the boards to help coax the animals into the front yard while Elisabeth tempted the pigs to follow her by dangling corn in front of their snouts. Once the last pig had been corralled back in, Anna closed the gate and slid her mitten back on.

"Tata has some tools in the wagon shed," Elisabeth said to the two men. "Help the Hagels finish the repairs. The pigs are fine for now."

The cousins nodded and did as instructed. Meanwhile, the girls filled their pails with dried corn kernels and began dropping small handfuls of the feed on the ground near the enclosures. The chickens, ducks, and geese began to quiet down.

Herr Hagel came running out, his face red with anger.

"I will *not* work with that crazy man!" he insisted.

Elisabeth had had enough. "Herr Hagel, that man is my cousin. He fought in the war. And whatever you may think of him, I know for one thing that he would not create a mess such as you and your son have. We need that pen fixed *now,* and since you and your son have done little to help, you must accept Georg's help."

"I *lost* two sons in that war, Elisabeth, and I know many in our village—including your fine father—who do not have problems. How do I know your crazy cousin won't swing a hammer at me and my last son and try to kill us?"

Elisabeth was dumb-founded. Were people that frightened of Georg? Was that what they were saying about him? The look of triumph on Herr Hagel's face at Elisabeth's silence fed her anger, and she found her words again.

"Let me put it to you this way, Herr Hagel. You and your

son promised my family that you would repair our pen. Either you complete your promise or the village will know that you are not a man of your word."

"I did not say I would repair it *with a crazy man*."

"You did not say without one either," Elisabeth replied. "It is your choice. Either you fulfill your promise and receive Jesus' blessing, or you do not and must go home, with Konrad, and confess your sins to our Lord."

With that, Elisabeth turned her back on Herr Hagel and focused her attention again on tempting the pigs into the poultry yard.

ELISABETH COULDN'T WAIT FOR THE EVENING TO BE OVER. Throughout cleanup, cooking, and dinner, she kept looking up at the crucifix, begging Jesus for one more moment of patience. Not only did she have to help herd the pigs back in to their pen and calm all the birds, but she and Anna had needed to change before starting supper because of how dirty and smelly their clothing had become. Elisabeth knew this meant there would be more laundry. Anna had a scowl on her face, because she, too, knew the extra work she would now have to help with.

Elisabeth had managed to hold in her anger all evening but she did not smile. The Hagels now stood at the door, after they had consumed a great deal of food, and continued to blame one another for the mess. If they didn't leave within two minutes, Elisabeth was certain she would have to pull the crucifix down from the wall and hold on to it to push down what she really wanted to tell this father and son.

Rosina had found Luki hiding under his bed, crying. "He kept saying it wasn't his fault," Rosina had told her sisters. Hearing that made Elisabeth's heart bleed for her young brother.

Konrad smiled at Elisabeth when she handed him his coat. But she did not return the smile.

"Thank you, Herr Hagel, for helping with the repairs," Mammi said, her voice tense and unnaturally polite.

Herr Hagel nodded in a way that said he was pleased with himself. "It was our honour, Frau Schuhmacher," he replied. "Had Konrad done his job better, of course, we would not have had the, um, difficulties that we did today."

"That was not my fault!" Konrad replied as he put his coat on.

"Do you always fight?" Rosina asked. Elisabeth couldn't scold Rosina for her question: she was fighting back an urge to chuckle herself.

"Children must obey their parents," Herr Hagel told her. He then looked down at Luki. "This young lad needs to learn to obey better, Frau Schuhmacher."

Elisabeth's anger began to push against her throat. *Please help me stay quiet, Jesus*, she prayed to herself.

Mammi replied. "He can be difficult, but boys will be boys, Herr Hagel. I'm certain you were no better."

"And I was disciplined accordingly," Herr Hagel replied, "as Konrad has been."

Elisabeth could no longer control her anger. "Herr Hagel, how dare you insult my mother! She has raised us well and continues to do so! It doesn't matter whose fault it was out there. What matters is that it was dealt with quickly. Need I remind you that *I* led the herding? If your son was raised so well, why did he not take charge so you could finish the work?"

Herr Hagel's mouth dropped open and he needed a moment to compose himself. "That is no way to speak to a man, Elisabeth."

"It is when he insults my family," she replied. After an uncomfortable pause, she changed her tone. "I really must start cleaning up the dishes now. Thank you again for your help. I'm sure we will see you at church on Sunday."

No sooner had the door closed behind the Hagels a few moments later when Mammi and Omama said in unison, "You're not marrying him." Elisabeth breathed a sigh of relief. Omama hobbled back to the kitchen table and sat down, while Mammi began rinsing dishes in the washing bowl and Elisabeth carried the remaining dishes from the table to Mammi.

"A good man looks after and protects his family," Mammi said. "You remember that, Luki."

Elisabeth's brother nodded.

"And he apologizes when he's made an error," Omama replied, as though what Elisabeth had just done had never happened. "No. He was a bad choice. We will find you someone else."

As happy as she was with this news, Elisabeth wondered if she was better off finding the right man herself. If Hagel Konrad was any sign of what Mammi and Omama thought would be a good match for Elisabeth, she might need to take matters into her own hands.

WHEN ALL HER SIBLINGS WERE TUCKED IN BED AND OMAMA was snoring in the guest bed in the back room, Elisabeth sat down at the kitchen table with her drawing book, a lantern, a slice of bread and butter, and a cup of tea. She wanted to draw the chaos that had transpired outside today, but if Tata wanted this book to show him everything that had happened in his absence, she wanted it to be filled with important memories.

Mammi emerged from the front room in her sleeping gown, her *haube* on, and her hair in a single braid down her back. Elisabeth placed her drawing pencil in her book and closed it.

"Would you like some bread?" she asked. "You hardly ate at supper tonight."

Mammi waved away the comment. "Today was more stress than planning my wedding was," she said. "Those Hagels will not be helping us in the future."

This time, Elisabeth didn't stifle her chuckle.

"It isn't funny, Elisabeth," Mammi admonished her, and Elisabeth dropped her smile right away. "You need a man who puts his family first. Hagel Samuel puts himself first, and his son is no different. A good man is in charge of his family, which is his source of pride. I knew Hagel Samuel was a proud man, but I did not know he would throw his own son under a horse's hooves to protect his pride. Konrad will follow in his footsteps." She shook her head. "No, he is not for you."

Mammi saw Elisabeth's book of drawings, pulled it toward her, and opened it up. She turned the first few pages and saw Elisabeth's drawings of the kitchen, Georg's hands pulling at Anna's mittens, and the wedding. She shook her head again as she closed it and stood up.

"Such a beautiful but useless gift," she muttered, and returned to the front room.

Elisabeth also didn't know why she felt compelled to draw. "What good is it?" she asked Jesus as she bit into her slice of bread and began sketching the back side of an envelope.

CHAPTER THIRTEEN

uliana sat in the change room, disappointed again. Supper had gone well, but after Aunt Anne offered to take Juliana to dance, Mom had accepted because she apparently had too much to do at work. *What's the point of being a manager if you can't leave when you want to?* Juliana wondered in anger. Moreover, Juliana had hoped to catch Jasmine before class, but one of the teachers had called in sick, and since Jasmine was in the studio's apprentice program, she'd been asked to supply.

"Today just sucks," she said to herself. She slid on her ballet shoes, pulled her leg warmers all the way up, and slipped into a tight-fitting ballet sweater. Miss Ambrosia, the ballet teacher, allowed students to wear warm-up clothing, but after barre, it all had to be removed.

Juliana walked out of the change room and almost got run over by a group of kids. *Is class already starting?* she wondered. But none of the other classes had come out yet. Juliana shrugged and was continuing on her way to go see the dancers from her group in the homework room when she heard muffled yelling coming from one of the music rooms. Juliana looked around at the other parents calmly waiting for their kids. No one seemed to bat an eyelash, so at first Juliana ignored the yelling, too. But as she continued to the homework room, the yelling didn't stop and Juliana felt that something was wrong. Who needed to yell that much at a student? As she neared the music room, she could hear some of the words.

"...she's too young!...What were you thinking...?"

Juliana stopped at the door and peeked in the window. A woman's back was turned to the door, her arms alternating between flying everywhere and parking on her hips. Now, Juliana could hear every word she was saying.

"What right do you have to tell the kids they can't move the way they want to? They're seven! She needs to explore her imagination! Or don't you have any? My daughter just started last year and you're already expecting her to be a prima ballerina!"

Juliana craned her neck and gasped: the woman was yelling at Jasmine. Juliana's new friend stood there like a statue, fear frozen on her face. Jasmine needed help, but what could Juliana do? The other teachers were still in class. Juliana hurried back down the short corridor to the reception desk. Unfortunately, Mrs. Laing and her office assistants were occupied with other parents. The woman's voice became louder. Juliana glanced at the men and women sitting in the waiting room. A few looked in the direction of the noise, but then they returned their attention to their devices.

How can they not care enough to get up and see what's going on?

Juliana rushed back to the music room and looked inside. The woman's gestures had become more frantic. Juliana had to help, but she didn't know what to do. Should she try to intervene? Who else was going to help if she didn't?

"My daughter *loves* dance! And because of you, she didn't smile all class!"

Juliana placed her hand on the doorknob.

"I pay lots of money to have the top teachers instruct her, and tonight she's left with a teenager!"

Juliana's hand stopped. No, another teenager would make things worse: this was way out of her control. She had to get help. She bolted down the hallway, turned the corner, and continued running to the last studio, where Miss Denise was teaching the seniors. Juliana burst into the studio. The dancers stopped, but the music kept blaring over the speakers.

Miss Denise placed her hands on her hips. "Juliana, you don't interrupt—"

"Jasmine really needs your help," she said. "Some mother is screaming at her."

A look of concern crossed Miss Denise's face. She instructed one of the dancers to restart the music while she looked into things. Juliana told her what she'd overheard as they rushed toward the music room. When they reached Jasmine, they heard the mother swearing at her. Without hesitation, Miss Denise swung the door open. Jasmine startled but then relaxed when she saw who it was.

"You do not speak to my students that way," Miss Denise said. "You talk to me. Juliana, Jasmine, you've got class shortly. Go get ready and close the door behind you."

As the two headed down the hallway to ballet, they could hear the mother yelling at Miss Denise, and Miss Denise in turn speaking firmly back to her. Heads turned and stared at the girls.

Sure, now they pay attention, Juliana thought. Once they were back in their change room, she asked Jasmine if she was all right.

Jasmine's answer came out cold, her eyes avoiding Juliana. "Yeah, I'm fine." She quickly switched her shoes.

"How can you be fine?" Juliana asked. Jasmine usually exuded a confidence that intimidated Juliana, but watching her scratch her head, adjust her hair, fiddle with her shoes, and twice drop a leg warmer, for the first time Juliana witnessed fear and agitation in her friend instead.

Jasmine continued to avert her gaze from Juliana. "You have to move on. What good is it dwelling on someone like that?" She took a swig of water before practically running out of the change room.

Juliana followed her, keeping pace. "She swore at you!" she said through clenched teeth. "No one deserves that!"

Jasmine stopped, and Juliana almost ran into her. "But I still have to move on. I refuse to let a mother who can't control her anger interfere with my training."

Jasmine picked up her pace and Juliana followed. "But how can you not be even a little upset by that?"

"Stop it, okay?" Jasmine said. They reached the studio and this time she bore her gaze into Juliana's eyes. "I have goals in life that I'm going to achieve. That mother is an absolute witch, and everyone knows she's like that. But if I'm going to pass my ballet exams this year and keep up my high scores in competition, I need to focus. The last thing I need is for you to keep reminding me about this."

The moment Jasmine stepped over the threshold and into the studio, her mood changed, as though she had entered onstage and was about to perform in front of a panel of judges. *How does she do that?* Juliana wondered. But something inside her told her that Jasmine wasn't fine. Miss Denise came down the hallway and Juliana indicated she wanted to speak with her.

"Are you okay?" Miss Denise asked.

Juliana nodded. "But I don't know if Jasmine is. She said she was fine, but something just doesn't feel right."

Miss Denise looked past Juliana and into the ballet studio, where Jasmine was already warming up.

"Thank you. You did the right thing coming to get me. I'll talk with Jasmine when she has a moment. But I know she often prefers time alone first, and if she can spend that time dancing, that helps her a lot."

Juliana understood exactly what Miss Denise meant.

CHAPTER FOURTEEN

It was Saturday, the most important day of the week after Sunday. Saturday was the day the girls and women in every German home in Semlak scrubbed the house from top to bottom. Right now, all three Schuhmacher daughters were working on the very bottom: smoothing out the little dents and holes in the dirt-and-chaff floor. Anna and Rosina were in the back room, on their hands and knees, with the carpets rolled back, rubbing at the wetted floor.

"That spot must be made perfectly smooth!" Omama ordered from her bed.

"I'm trying!" Rosina said.

"Not hard enough!" Omama countered.

"She is learning, Omama, I promise. Just after Christmas, it took us a lot longer to finish this room than it did today," Anna said in her sister's defence.

"You're not done yet."

"Almost. And we're getting faster because Rosina's getting faster."

Inwardly, Elisabeth smiled. Her sisters had been on their absolute best behaviour the last couple of days—of course, only when Omama was around. But that didn't matter. It meant that the box of dried corn kernels had stayed in the cupboard.

Elisabeth stood in the front room with the special watering can used to gently wet the floor before she could begin rubbing away at the divots and crevices that had made their way into the floor over the course of the week. The chairs had been lifted onto the table, and the blankets folded up onto the beds so she could reach underneath and get out any bugs that might have made their home in there over the past week.

Luki sat uncharacteristically quietly on his bed, tossing a rubber ball up and down while Elisabeth gently poured the water from the can onto the floor, creating the outline of a simple flower.

"You're quiet," she said to her brother, whom Mammi again had sent inside. "Is everything all right?"

Luki didn't respond. Elisabeth knelt down on the ground and began rubbing.

"Anna!" Omama reprimanded. "You missed a spot under my bed!"

Elisabeth rolled her eyes. She could only imagine what Peter-Bátschi and his family must have faced with his mother in their home.

"I'm very sorry, Omama. Let me get that one."

Elisabeth felt horrible for her sisters, but what else were they supposed to do? Mammi would be embarrassed if her children fought with her mother, and even if the siblings' wildest dream could ever come true—kicking Omama out—the entire village would talk about them and Mammi could lose her customers.

Jesus, please send Omama home, she prayed. It was the only request she believed she could make without harming her family's reputation. Then she returned her attention to her brother. "Luki, you can talk to me." She looked up at him as she rubbed at the floor, and he finally stopped playing with his ball.

"Are you going to marry Konrad?" he asked.

Elisabeth stopped. "Is that why you're so quiet? You're worried about that?"

He kept his eyes focused on his ball as he nodded. "He yells more than Omama does." Elisabeth stroked his arm and then returned to rubbing the floor. "No," she replied. "I will not."

Luki's eyes lit up. "Are you sure?"

Elisabeth smiled and nodded and Luki began bouncing

up and down on his bed and laughing, the crunching hay in the mattress sounding just as happy as he did. Elisabeth couldn't help but laugh, too. She was also happy that Konrad would not be part of her future.

JESUS HAD ANSWERED ELISABETH'S PRAYER! PETER-BÁTSCHI had come by after lunch and had said that he would pick up Omama before supper to take her home. Sophie-Néni had managed to give their house a decent cleaning, and he had apologized to his mother for the state of his family and had promised to do better.

A knock on the door made Elisabeth rush to answer it and she let her uncle in, a big grin on her face.

"It's about time he got here," Omama grumbled as she came into the kitchen from the back room.

Peter-Bátschi kissed Elisabeth and Mammi on each cheek, patted the younger girls on the head, shook Luki's hand, and then nodded to his mother. His cheeks were red, but Elisabeth was certain it wasn't because of the cold: he only lived a few houses away so he couldn't have been outside long enough for his cheeks to turn red. His face was flushed clearly because of the entire situation.

"My suitcase is in the back room," Omama declared. Elisabeth took a step to get it, and Omama grabbed her wrist. "My son can do that," she said. Peter-Bátschi wiped his boots off well and retrieved Omama's belongings. "I must say," Omama continued, "it's easier to live in a household where the father isn't around at all than one where the father ignores his family."

Peter-Bátschi's face turned an even deeper shade of red, and although Elisabeth found her uncle's reaction a little funny, Omama's comments hurt her. If Tata had been around, none of this week's chaos would have happened, Luki would have had a father at home to show him how to be a good man, and Elisabeth would still have had her teacher. As much as Elisabeth tried to be honest with her family and friends, and as much as she appreciated when others were kind and honest with her, too, she sometimes wished some words were never said.

"But your family needs me," Omama declared to her son. "If only to make sure you spend less time with your friends and more with your family, like I raised you to do." She swatted him on the shoulder and hobbled out the door.

"She didn't even say thank you," Rosina said. "You're supposed to say thank you when someone does something nice for you."

Peter-Bátschi nodded in agreement and tipped his hat. "But I will say thank you for your help this week." He sighed. "And I'm sorry."

Now Mammi whacked him on the shoulder. "Get your family in order and stop leaving messes for the rest of us to clean up after you." Elisabeth tried to stifle a chuckle, but Anna and Rosina failed at it. Mammi faced Elisabeth, her expression serious. "This is also the kind of man you don't want."

Peter-Bátschi's face remained red as he turned and hurried out the door.

"Peter!" Mammi shouted after him. "Modr's suitcase!"

He reappeared, grabbed it, and disappeared. After Mammi closed the door, all four children giggled.

"It's not funny," Mammi said. "He's an embarrassment to the Braun name. Who can't look after his own family?" Her steely eyes focused on Luki, and he ducked behind Elisabeth. "Yes, that's right," Mammi said. "You'll be living with me for as long as I live."

The three sisters burst out in laughter.

EVERYONE WAS IN BED, EXCEPT ELISABETH. SHE HAD promised Mammi she wouldn't stay up late but she needed some time to think. Although Mammi's face had showed she disapproved of such wasted time, she had mumbled, "If it's God's will that you have this gift, then...fine."

Elisabeth completed her sketch of an envelope in her book. She drew it to show the envelope being opened by someone, hoping to remind Tata of the anticipation they would both feel in that moment, eager to read words from someone they loved. Would she someday write in a letter the name of the man she would marry? Or would she instead tell Tata story after story of men she did not like?

With two POWs returned, the war had taken fifty-one young men from the village, leaving more girls and widows vying for the ones left. Several more soldiers were still stationed in Budapest, hopefully to return in the coming months. Was Konrad perhaps one of the better men left?

Even though finding a husband was exciting for Elisabeth, after this past week, she could sense how unsettling the prospect was for her siblings. It had never occurred to her that the fear of her leaving was so strong in their minds. Perhaps it was best to leave it alone for now? But the thought of having her own house to run as she pleased was too exciting to just let go. She also knew that once she turned twenty, she would have a harder time finding someone.

What news would Elisabeth's next letter to Tata contain?

CHAPTER FIFTEEN

The following morning, Juliana stared at her phone.

Should I or shouldn't I?

She wanted to call Jasmine and see how she was feeling, but Jasmine's retort played over and over in her mind: *The last thing I need is for you to keep reminding me about this.* But Miss Denise had said that Jasmine often needed to dance before she was ready to talk. What if Jasmine wanted a friend now the way Juliana could have used one the night before?

She's got friends from school, Juliana thought. *Probably people she's known for years. Would I want some new girl calling me up while I was talking things out with Rachel?*

On her night table was Omama's book of drawings, opened to the envelope. Juliana had asked Opa again what might have been in it, but he only repeated the same thing: that it was likely about a letter either from his grandfather to his mother or vice versa.

She draws it so realistically, I want to rip it open and find out what's inside. Juliana sighed. This book contained so many mysteries, and she didn't know if she would ever solve even half of them.

But she would have had to wait...how long did letters take to travel back then? Juliana thought for a few moments and then searched for the answer on her phone. *A couple of weeks at least?* That was a long time to wait for someone you cared about to help you with any problems you had. She reconsidered her own dilemma. If she had met a new girl in class, and that girl had helped her, wouldn't Juliana find it nice if that girl asked how she was doing, even if the timing wasn't convenient? Moreover, Jasmine struck Juliana as someone who didn't like asking for help. What if she wanted someone to talk to right now but didn't want to say anything? That meant Juliana wasn't being a good friend by not asking.

Worst case scenario, she won't answer me and I can ask her about it tonight, Juliana thought. She wouldn't have to wait for weeks for her message to arrive and then several more weeks to get an answer.

She opened up her messaging app and stared at it for a few more moments as she wondered just what to ask. Thankfully, the right question appeared in her mind.

Did you want to practice today? I'm behind because of my exams and could use a practice partner.

She stared at her phone, hoping for a reply. Only after her hands got stiff did she realize she'd been gripping her phone tightly for several minutes. "Several minutes feels like several weeks," she said aloud. She glanced over at the old book. "How did you manage?" Then her phone beeped and she almost squealed in delight. It was Jasmine.

What time?

Juliana quickly typed back. *Any time. Now? After lunch? Your place or mine?* She waited, and soon enough, the three dots began pulsating as Jasmine typed.

Now's good. Your place.

Awesome!

Juliana quickly typed in her address, dropped her phone onto her bed and jumped up to get ready for Jasmine's visit. She looked at herself in the mirror and smiled. "The first time I'm having someone over!" she said to her happy reflection, and she jumped up and down, the nervous energy rushing into her body and needing an immediate exit. Her phone beeped again and she picked it up.

Thanks about last night. And sorry. It wasn't personal.

No worries. Let's just dance and leave the rest alone. Kk? Bring tap board.

There in 20.

Juliana responded with a thumbs-up emoji, tucked the

phone into her pants pocket in case Jasmine texted again, and began double-checking her room, the kitchen, and the rec room for any unsightly messes.

Juliana rushed to open the door. "Hey!" she said to Jasmine. "Come on in!" Jasmine smiled and stepped inside with her tap board, which made it a tight squeeze for the two of them on the landing. "Here, let me take that," Juliana offered and rushed it into the basement, placing it next to hers.

"There's no hurry!" Jasmine called down.

Juliana giggled. "Sorry! It's the first time I've had a friend over. Well, here, not the first time ever! I'm a little excited!" She bounded up the stairs, yanked Jasmine's coat out of her hands, and hung it in the hallway closet. Jasmine followed Juliana into the kitchen.

"You really wear your emotions on your sleeve, don't you?" Jasmine said, a slightly bemused expression on her face.

Juliana had never thought about it before. "I just need to get my energy out, I guess. Something to drink?" Her heart still beating a million miles a minute, she grabbed a glass before Jasmine could even answer.

"Sure," Jasmine said with a laugh and pulled out a chair. "Just water, though."

"My favourite," Juliana said and poured two glasses. "I'm glad you could come over. It can get pretty lonely here."

"Your parents not home?"

"No. Mom's at work and Dad's on a drive to Georgia. Opa's here, though, but he's in his room right now, probably watching some news or talk show."

An awkward silence settled in the kitchen. Juliana wanted to ask about last night, but she didn't want to upset Jasmine either. If something was bothering Jasmine, Juliana wanted her new friend to know that she could talk about it.

"Thanks for coming over," she said to break the silence. "I'm so behind and need to catch up."

Jasmine swallowed her mouthful of water. "I know why you wanted to get together today. You asked me over to make sure I was okay."

Juliana blushed. "Am I that obvious?"

"Yup."

"Sorry."

"But I'm fine. Mrs. Orzel is one of those crazy dance moms who thinks her child is going to make it big just because she's cute." She drank the last sip of water and set her glass down. "Downstairs?"

"Yup!" Juliana finished hers and then led the way. When they were halfway down the stairs, Opa came out of his room.

"Hello," he said. "Who are you?"

"Opa, this is Jasmine. She's from my new dance school," Juliana explained. "We're going to practice."

"Hi," Jasmine said, a friendly smile on her face.

"It's nice to meet Yulika's friends. I'm Peter. Have fun!" Opa said and let the girls come down the stairs before he went up.

"Yulika?" Jasmine asked. "Is that your real name or something?"

"No," Juliana said. "It's his nickname for me. It's either that or Yuliana. He doesn't like putting the *j* sound at the front of it for some reason."

They entered the rec room. "He seems really sweet," Jasmine said. "How has he been?"

Juliana shrugged. "I think normal for where he's at. I wish my parents were home more often, though. Lately, I feel like I'm the one who's supposed to look after him. I mean, I knew Dad would be gone for long stretches, but I honestly thought Mom would be home more often."

Juliana sat on the floor in a wide straddle to stretch her hamstrings and inner thigh muscles, and Jasmine stretched into a deep lunge.

"Sounds pretty peaceful, though," Jasmine said.

"It can be, but when both Mom and Dad are home, I've got two parents and a grandfather watching me, and then it seems like I can't do anything right."

"I know the feeling," Jasmine replied.

As they continued to warm up and chat, something in Juliana dissipated. It took her a few moments to figure out what it was and why, but then she got it: the stress of the past month had finally disappeared, and the reason was Jasmine's visit. It felt good to finally have a friend over. She couldn't wait to find a time for Meghan and Shawna, but that would have to wait until next week, when school started again. Juliana was certain she'd be sleeping and practicing a lot the rest of this week.

Juliana's ears were wide open.

"Semlak wasn't backwards," Opa insisted.

"Really?" Mom countered. "You lived on dirt floors and had an outhouse and a well in the 1950s."

"It was that bad?" Dad asked.

"You have no idea," Mom replied. "And then the Communists came and things got even worse. Some rural areas in Romania still don't have indoor toilets."

"But we eventually had floorboards and a range. I believe Mammi actually had a Vesta after she married."

"A what?" Juliana asked.

"Vesta was the brand name for these massive, ugly ranges that eventually replaced the brick-and-lime ovens they had," Mom answered. "Modr could never stop talking about it when I was a kid. She kept saying how much more advanced things were in Temeswar, where she grew up."

The entire family was dining out at a steakhouse in Kitchener. Mom hadn't eaten there in years, and so she had begged everyone to drive halfway through town to humour her. Opa was sharp as a whistle this Friday evening, so Juliana had asked to hear more about Semlak. She hadn't intended to unleash a debate, though.

"We eventually put floorboards in," Opa said. "And Mammi painted beautiful designs on the walls, something that became the fashion over there and never here."

"Well, I guess you have a point. Here, wallpaper became the fashion, and look where that got us."

Juliana chuckled. The fuzzy, floral wallpaper in her room certainly proved Mom's point. But her thoughts whipped back to Opa's comments. Omama did more than just draw in a notebook? But what were Communists? And if Omama had an outhouse and no running water, where did everyone shower? A thousand more questions ran through Juliana's head, jamming her train of thought and preventing her from asking even just one.

"And we had friendships that lasted years and even generations," Opa said. "You only moved out of Semlak because of war, to go to America, or to go to God. Everyone knew everyone."

"Tata, by the time you went to school there, people were leaving to move to the city."

"But not my friends."

Dad took a sip of his beer. "It does sound nice, though. Something comforting about knowing everyone."

"He's making it sound nice," Mom said. "Everyone knew everyone's business. *Everyone* knew your life and *everyone* judged you for it."

"They made sure you behaved properly," Opa insisted. "And if you needed money, your friends lent it you. You didn't have to waste money getting money from a bank."

"You had a credit union! Don't tell me no one borrowed from the credit union."

"But your friends still borrowed you money."

"'Lent,' Tata, it's 'lent' in English."

"Fine. And weddings were beautiful! Everyone brought their own dishes, all the family and close friends cooked—"

"The *women* cooked and didn't get paid."

"The men butchered the pigs!"

"And that was it!" Mom's phone beeped. "Just a sec, Tata." She pulled it out of her purse, read the message, and then began texting.

"Seriously, Mom?" Juliana said. "You won't let me text at the dinner table."

Not taking her eyes off her phone, Mom said, "You don't manage fifty people, all of them wanting your attention and relying on you to support their families. Sorry, I've got to call them. This can't wait." She left the table.

"This is the most I've heard about any of this," Dad said, apparently just as intrigued about Semlak as Juliana. "Katy rarely brings it up. You were saying, Peter?" And then his phone rang. He checked the number. "Sorry—it's my boss."

Opa raised his eyebrows. "On a Friday night?"

"Every ride I do I get paid for," Dad said. "I'm new in the company, and that means I don't get to ignore my boss when he has a trip for me." Dad answered the phone and also left the table.

Juliana watched as her parents walked out of the eating area toward the lobby.

"These phones you all have," Opa said. "They do nothing but cause trouble."

"Not entirely," Juliana said. "They do let me stay in touch with Rachel and my friends."

Opa shook his head in dismay at her parents. "This would have never happened back at home. When everyone sat down to eat, everyone talked to each other." He paused as he seemed to remember something. "Although I remember Mammi saying that when she was a child, she wasn't allowed to talk at the table."

"This conversation was nice, I have to admit," Juliana said.

Opa reached over and grabbed her hand. "Your parents do love you, a lot, Yulika. It's why they do what they do." He let go and leaned back in his chair. "But these phones...are they really necessary?"

An idea popped into Juliana's head. Her own phone was in her jacket, which was hanging over the back of her chair. Memories seemed to be crystal clear to him right now, and if his memory was indeed fading, then…

"What were you saying about Omama's painting?" Juliana said as she discreetly pulled her phone out, turned on the voice recorder, and pretended to adjust the serviette on the table while she lay the phone just next to it.

"That her painting was very beautiful. She would paint lovely flowers on our walls—it had finally become fashionable between the wars to decorate the white walls, and she continued it when we returned to Semlak when I was a child."

"Wait. You mean you weren't born there?"

"I was born there. But then Mammi moved away to Temeswar for a little." His eyes began to lose focus and he appeared to be drifting into his memories. "No, your mother is wrong," he continued. "It was a small community, and the only place Mammi felt comfortable raising her young child without his father. Yes, they gossiped about her—even I heard the rumours once I started attending school—but everyone made sure I was taken care of."

"You had no father?" Juliana leaned forward, eager to hear more.

"I'm back," Mom said, and Juliana almost jumped. Really? Now? Mom couldn't talk on the phone longer? Juliana slid the serviette over her phone and moved both items on to her lap where she could turn off the recording app. "What were you talking about?" Mom asked.

Opa thought for a moment and then shrugged. Had he really forgotten?

"What?" Mom asked. "Was it some kind of secret?" She smiled, and Juliana forced a smile back.

"I asked Opa to tell me more about Omama's paintings."

Opa's eyes lit up. "They were so beautiful, Katy. I wish you could've seen them. But is everything all right at work? I mean, for them to call you on your night off…?"

For the rest of the meal, Juliana couldn't take her thoughts away from what Opa had said. He had no father? Or had his father maybe died? If Omama returned home after choosing to move away, then something horrible must have happened, otherwise why else would she do it? *Or, maybe she just missed her family*, Juliana thought. After what had happened this past month to her, she could relate.

CHAPTER SIXTEEN

Rosina sat dutifully at the table in the front room, her tongue stuck out as though its presence would help her finish her third row of knitting. Herr Blum had returned to school, so both Anna and Luki were finally back in class.

"I'm taking food out to Mammi!" Elisabeth called to her, and Rosina nodded, not taking her eyes off her handiwork.

Elisabeth switched out her shoes for her boots and wrapped a shawl around her shoulders—the weather had warmed up a little, but not enough for her to be able to leave her shawl behind. She carried a cup of tea in one hand and a plate with buttered bread and a few slices of salami in the other.

The wind blew fiercely along the side of the house, and

Elisabeth hoped Mammi wasn't too cold in the workshop. Although Tata had built it into the summer kitchen at the back of the house so it was sheltered, they didn't have the time or money to build any kind of heat source into it. Only the few gas lamps Mammi had in there provided any warmth. Maybe Elisabeth should have brought Mammi an extra blanket, too? But when Elisabeth neared the door, a more immediate worry appeared: she could hear Mammi throwing up. Elisabeth's heart began to race. Had the Spanish flu the postman had talked about gotten its grip on their mother?

Elisabeth burst into the workshop to see her mother leaning over a bowl. "Mammi? What's wrong?"

Mammi's eyes pierced Elisabeth's. "Nothing is wrong! What are you doing here?"

Taken aback by Mammi's flash of anger, Elisabeth lost her words.

Mammi saw the food in Elisabeth's hand. "Leave that here and go."

As Elisabeth set the plate down on the workbench, her voice finally returned. "But you're sick...You need to rest."

"I'm fine. Now go and look after the day's chores."

"But..."

"Go! You have chores to do!"

Mammi's cheeks puffed out and she gestured for Elisabeth to get out of the workshop. Just as Elisabeth closed the door, she heard Mammi get sick again.

ONCE SHE RETURNED TO THE LIVING AREA OF THE HOUSE, Elisabeth heard Rosina crying. It was only mid-morning and she was beginning to wonder what else could happen today.

"What's wrong?" she asked her sister.

Rosina slammed her knitting on the table. "I can't do it!"

Really? Elisabeth asked Jesus as He hung on His cross. *Mammi's sick and now I have to deal with my impatient little sister?* Elisabeth took a deep breath and, after putting on her house shoes, walked over to her sister and stroked her shoulder. "I keep telling you that crocheting is easier to learn when you're young. If you would listen to me, you wouldn't be so upset."

But her words had the opposite effect on Rosina. She clutched her knitting needles in her little hands again. "I'm knitting!" she shouted, and within moments her tongue was again sticking out between her lips, trying to help her get the needle with yarn wrapped around it back through the loop.

Exasperated, Elisabeth decided to move her list of chores around and do some ironing; she needed something to calm her down. Back in the kitchen, she lay two table-cloths over the table, got the iron from the kitchen cabinet and filled it with simmering coals from the oven. She grabbed a pair of Luki's pants out of the basket of dry laundry. While the iron warmed up, Elisabeth laid out the pants and carefully folded the legs lengthwise.

As the iron glided up and down the soft linen, Elisabeth's thoughts kept turning to her mother. How could she be sick but fine? All last week, Mammi had seemed fine except when the pigs got out and she had held her hand over her stomach. Then Elisabeth realized something. "She barely ate all week," Elisabeth said to Jesus on the crucifix. "She worked alone often, couldn't help with the animals on Wednesday, and she's sent Luki inside several times, even to polish shoes. Has she been sick all this time?" The more Elisabeth recalled the events of the week, the more concerned she became. She set the iron on the stove, changed her shoes once more and grabbed her shawl.

"I need to ask Mammi something!" she shouted back to Rosina.

"I'm concentrating!" Rosina shouted back, and Elisabeth took that to mean her sister had heard her.

Once outside the door to the workshop, Elisabeth stopped for a moment to listen to Mammi, who was tapping away on a shoe. Elisabeth entered, but she almost recoiled from the smell of vomit in the air.

"What is it now?" Mammi growled at her.

This time, Elisabeth stood her ground. "You're sick, Mammi. You told me—"

"I told you I was fine. Now go!"

Without another word, Mammi returned to her work, ignoring any pleas from her daughter.

ELISABETH STOOD AT THE STOVE IN THEIR EMPTY HOUSE, where she had been steeping chamomile flowers in boiling water for twenty minutes to make a concentrated tea. She didn't know what was wrong with Mammi, but she knew she was having problems with her stomach. She wanted to make Mammi a tea and hopefully convince her to at least come inside and rest for a bit. She had sent Rosina over to a neighbour's house to play. With the house now empty, Mammi could rest without anyone else in the family knowing she was ill.

Elisabeth removed the tea from the burner, sliced some bread and sprinkled it with paprika. She placed a lid on the tea and headed out back to fetch Mammi.

When she opened the door, Mammi slammed her fist on the table. "What now?!"

Elisabeth remained calm. "I've made some tea for you, some bread and paprika, and sent Rosina to the Bartolfs on the corner to play," she said, not wavering under her mother's anger this time. "You need to rest. I can scrub down the workshop for you, organize your materials if you need that done...Whatever you wanted to do this afternoon by the time everyone got home, I'll look after it as best I can. But you're sick, Mammi." Tears welled up in Elisabeth's eyes. "We can't lose you, too. You've hardly eaten this past week, and then you wouldn't help with the animals, and you looked sick but I was too busy being angry at the Hagels and forgot about it. But now I see it clearly. You need to let me help."

She wiped the tears away from her face, ashamed that she was crying at all. Mammi hadn't even cried when Tata had left.

"You worry too much about me," Mammi said. Her tone had softened. "If I were ever to get sick, I would tell you. I am not sick."

"Then at least come inside, where it's warm, and rest for a bit. Maybe we should ask Georg to build a little stove for in here. I'm certain I can offer to help him and Eva with something in return."

Mammi took a long look at her daughter, and Elisabeth stared back. She was not going to let her mother's anger push her down. Not this time, at least.

To Elisabeth's relief, Mammi nodded and stood up. "But just to warm up and eat, then I'm coming back out here," she said.

In the kitchen, Mammi stood by the oven, warming her hands, while Elisabeth set the tea and food on the table. Once both had sat down, though, Elisabeth continued pressing for an answer.

"Nobody is 'not sick' and throws up," she said. "Something is wrong with you."

Mammi glanced to the front room and then the door. Elisabeth couldn't figure out what was going on. What kind of illness could be so humiliating except for the kinds that robbed you of your memory and control?

"You're not old enough to know this yet, but, very well, I will answer you," Mammi said.

"I'm almost a woman," Elisabeth insisted.

Mammi nodded. "Yes, you are, but not yet. You *cannot* repeat this to anyone, including your sisters or brother or Maria. Is that understood?" Mammi took a tiny bite of the bread. "I am expecting a child, Elisabeth, and this one is very difficult."

The news shocked Elisabeth. A child? Why would God make Mammi a mother again when Tata wasn't home? Or was God doing this so Tata would have to return home sooner? But then the family wouldn't have a shingle roof, and Elisabeth might not be able to marry well if her dowry wasn't big enough. And what if Mammi died when she was about to receive the baby from God?

Elisabeth remembered Mammi's words from the evening she and Omama had discussed Elisabeth's readiness for a husband: *Elisabeth still has much to learn.*

Elisabeth didn't realize until now just how true that was.

CHAPTER SEVENTEEN

Juliana was jumping up and down in jazz choreography class.

"You get excited easily, don't you?" Jasmine said.

Juliana nodded her head fast. "It's costume day!"

Jasmine raised an eyebrow. "Did you not have costumes in Calgary?"

Juliana stopped jumping. "You people really think we live in a different country out there, don't you? Of course we had costumes. But I always love trying them on for the first time."

Miss Denise entered the studio, followed by Mrs. Laing, their arms full with black costumes in plastic garment bags. They hung them on a barre, and then Mrs. Laing walked out again.

"So, what do you think?" Miss Denise asked, holding one up.

Juliana thought her body was going to explode from all the excitement. The bodice piece was black, with wispy silver accents sewn randomly around it. The broad shoulder straps flowed into a v-neck and the bottom of the bodice extended into bike shorts. Over the hanger, she saw long, black gloves.

"Each of you gets a hat," Miss Denise said as Mrs. Laing reappeared with a stack of bowler hats. "Make sure you take the elastic that's pinned to your costume tag and have your moms sew it on."

She then began calling out each student's name, and Juliana kept hopping on the spot, waiting for hers. By the time the first fifteen had left to get changed, though, Juliana worried that maybe she'd been forgotten.

Wouldn't be the first time this year, she thought dryly.

"Mackenzie...Isaac...Savannah..."

Juliana stopped hopping. Was this really happening to her on one of the best days of the year? But to her relief, once everyone had left, there was indeed one costume still hanging on the barre.

"I need to talk to you for a moment," Miss Denise said.

Maybe this wasn't going to be one of the best days of the year. Juliana's palms began to sweat.

"I'm sorry I haven't spoken to you about what happened with Jasmine earlier this week."

Juliana gulped. Was she about to get into trouble?

Miss Denise shook her head in disbelief. "I can't believe that mother had the gall to talk to one of my students that way. She insisted last year that her daughter wear pigtails on stage at the recital instead of the ponytail she was supposed to wear because she swore ponytails made her daughter's head look big." Miss Denise rolled her eyes. "The poor girl was so embarrassed that she almost didn't go on stage. Anyway, I wanted to say again thank you for getting me. You saved your friend from a very high-maintenance customer."

Juliana's elation rose so fast inside her at the compliment that she now couldn't move.

Miss Denise continued. "Every studio has parents like that, so that's nothing new. But I'm telling you this because I know you wanted to join the apprentice program this year. I'd told your mom I wanted you to get used to the studio first, and it looks like it was a good thing. Your mom tells me that January was particularly hard on you."

"You talked with my mom?"

"Of course. We've been talking on the phone each week to make sure you're doing okay. We'll continue that for this month, and then we'll see if it's needed afterwards."

Juliana wasn't sure if she should be happy that her mom was taking part in her life or creeped out that she was spying on her. She didn't have time to decide, though: Miss Denise handed Juliana her costume.

"Keep up that kind of attitude, Juliana, and I'll be more than happy to put you in the apprentice program next year."

The news excited Juliana so much that she was again speechless, but her grin reached from ear to ear. Miss Denise smiled back. "Now get going, or you're going to hold up the group."

Juliana grand-jétéd out of the studio and ran to the change room.

"So, what courses are you registered in?" Meghan asked.

Juliana's new semester had begun, and she sat at a table in the Eby Heights cafeteria with Meghan and Shawna.

"English and math in the morning, and then science and geography after lunch." Juliana bit into her hummus-and-chicken sandwich.

"What teachers?" Meghan asked.

Juliana pointed to her full mouth, then pulled out her phone and opened her calendar app.

"You have your classes entered in your calendar?" Meghan asked incredulously. Even Shawna looked surprised.

Juliana swallowed her food. "Everything's in here. See?" She turned the phone so her new friends could see her schedule. Shawna took it out of her hand, a look of surprise still on her face.

"How can you handle all this?" she asked, her voice quiet as always.

"I just do it."

"You don't get stressed?" She handed the phone to Meghan so she could see it, too.

Juliana shrugged. Sure, she had been stressed in January, but that was a one-off situation. A packed schedule was nothing new for her, and concentrating on four courses in one semester would probably even be easier to manage than the eight courses she took every day in Calgary.

"Okay, let's see," Meghan said as she scrolled through Juliana's calendar. "You've got Ms. Lee for English. I had her last semester. She made Shakespeare feel like a death sentence. Gulminska for math...she's okay, nothing special, but I don't have her. Then Mr. Schmidt for science this afternoon. Hey, so do I! I hear he's awesome. Oh, and Ms. Haseltine again, for geography. Me, too! Hey, you have her, too, don't you, Shawna?"

Shawna nodded.

"I liked her," Juliana said. "She was weird but somehow I liked her."

"She actually makes you feel welcome in class," Shawna said.

"This is awesome," Meghan said. "We've got our afternoon classes together!"

Juliana's phone buzzed. Meghan handed it back to her. "A message from Rachel...?" she said.

Rachel was supposed to be in class. Juliana quickly looked at the message.

I need to talk to you NOW.

"Um, sorry, but I'd better call her," Juliana said and texted back.

"Who's Rachel?" Meghan asked.

"My best friend from back home. Something's up, or she wouldn't be texting at this time."

"It's lunch, though," Meghan said.

"Not in Calgary. Two hour time difference?"

"Oh, yeah, right."

Juliana left her lunch at her table and sought out a quieter corner in the cafeteria. She dialled.

Rachel was sobbing as she answered.

"Rachel! What's wrong?"

"Mom was in a car accident on her way to work."

"Oh my god, I'm so sorry! How's she doing?"

Rachel couldn't stop crying.

"Deep breaths," Juliana said. "I know I'm not there in person, but I'm with you. How's she doing?"

She could hear Rachel breathing into the phone as she tried to calm down enough to speak.

"Juliana, Mom's on life support."

Juliana felt like a powerful hand had clamped itself around her heart and had begun to squeeze.

"Rachel, oh my god, oh my god, oh my god!" Juliana shook her free hand to release the jittery, horrible energy now coursing through her. She forced herself to take deep breaths now, too.

"I don't know what to do," Rachel said. "Dad's coming to pick me up right now. I probably have to stay with him, which is fine, but..." Her voice trailed off.

How on earth could Juliana help Rachel from this distance?

"Jules, I love her, and I don't know if I've ever said that to her."

If there was one thing Juliana wanted more now than anything, it was to be by Rachel's side.

Juliana thought again about her great-grandmother. If Omama's father had ever written her that he was ill, she wouldn't know until his next letter whether or not he was even alive. No phone, no email, just letters. How did she deal with situations like that? All Juliana had to do now was jump into a plane and fly to her best friend. She could be there in a matter of hours. If she was allowed, which she knew would never happen. *It's unfair to be so far away!* she thought angrily.

But her anger wouldn't help Rachel. No. Juliana

couldn't share that with her best friend who needed her more now than ever. Instead, Rachel needed to hear what she always told Juliana.

"Rachel, it'll be fine. I promise we'll get through this."

But was that a promise Juliana could keep?

SETTING THE RECORD STRAIGHT

Between Worlds tells a completely fictional contemporary story together with a story that is historical fiction. In the historical part of the book, I've taken facts about life in a previous time and included them in a fictional story. In writing novels, the story always comes first (because otherwise this would be a history textbook), so this section explains any facts that may have been changed to fit the story, and adds some more background to the story. If you have any questions about what you've read in this or any of the other books in the series, ask away! My contact information is in the section "Stay in Touch!"

GETTING HELP WITH RESEARCH

The most difficult aspect of writing this series is accessing information written in Hungarian or Romanian. In addition to English, I speak and read German, but that only takes me so far. Through an online skills marketplace, I found two researchers who have helped me considerably with finding out more details about these times. This book only scratches the surface of what they found, but you will certainly read more in upcoming books.

MARRIAGE IN SEMLAK

In *Between Worlds 2: The Distance*, we followed Elisabeth as she helped a cousin with wedding preparations and were introduced to Georg and his young wife, Eva. My information for marriage in this time period comes from several sources: The book *Semlak* by Georg Schmidt, and recollections from my own great-grandparents who came from a different German settlement in a different region.

In his book, Schmidt explains that divorce was extremely exceptional in Semlak, and that young women married as early as fourteen, though sixteen was more the norm. Young men usually waited until after their required military service, although I haven't fully researched that aspect of village life yet. Schmidt further writes that engagements in Semlak were a mix of attraction and planning: young men and women were drawn to each other but then were carefully supervised; if they chose to marry, their parents had to approve.

How young couples came together in these German communities in Eastern Europe varied, and this is what I brought into the series. One of my great-grandmothers, Katharina, was born in 1910 in a village that today is located in Serbia. She told me a long time ago that she and my great-grandfather, Sebastian, were brought together by a matchmaker of sorts. She was, so far as I can remember, supposed to marry another man, but he became seriously ill, so he was no longer "in the running." In addition, Sebastian was a furrier (he worked with animal furs), which was important to Katharina because it meant she wouldn't have to work as hard as the farmers' wives did. And I still remember her light chuckle when I turned sixteen and she told me she was married by that age. (I didn't marry for another fourteen years.)

However, wars change things, as you'll see with the series. As far as marriage goes, by the time Katharina and Sebastian's daughter, Mary, married my grandfather, John, in 1950, it was definitely for love: you can see it in one of their wedding photos. In addition, my grandmother was eighteen by then, and my grandfather twenty-one. Marrying in my family happened later with each successive generation.

GETTING THE NEWS

The mailman did indeed come into town weekly, beat his drum to get attention, announce the week's headlines, and deliver the mail. Three of the four headlines used in this book were discovered by one of the researchers I hired in Romania. She had found digitized copies of *Românul*, a daily from Arad, the main city in Arad County, which Semlak belonged to. The headlines came from editions from February 10, 12, and 15, 1920. If you read Romanian, you can read the newspaper here: http://dspace.bcucluj.ro/handle/123456789/15738.

The fourth headline (about Romania being victorious and withdrawing from Hungary) is fictional, but the historical event is fact. Whereas most of us in North America celebrated the end of World War I on November 11, 1918, and have been doing so for more than a hundred years now, for many in Europe, war continued. On November 13, 1918, the Romanian army crossed into Transylvania, which was then still part of Hungary. Military events did not begin until April 1919 and they lasted until August of that year. Romanian troops occupied Budapest, Hungary's capital, until 1920. You'll find more information about the Hungarian-Romanian war on Wikipedia.

POWS

POWs, or prisoners of war, were soldiers caught and imprisoned by their enemies. Both sides of the war took prisoners, and treatment of these prisoners varied considerably. Many POWs were repatriated (i.e., returned to their own countries) relatively soon after the end of World War I. However, Russia was undergoing a lot of turmoil: from mid-1914 until 1922, three separate governments ruled the massive country, each one with their own opinion of how POWs should be treated. In addition, a civil war raged in Russia from 1917-1920, making repatriation of these POWs even more difficult. The last POWs were sent home in 1922, three years after the war ended. You can read more about WWI POWs in Russia here: https://encyclopedia.1914-1918-online.net/article/prisoners_of_war_russian_empire

I don't know if any Semlakers were prisoners of war in WWI, but Schmidt does confirm in his book that fifty-one German men from the village died in the conflict. The war killed many sons, brothers, and fathers, and Semlak was not spared from that tragedy.

A QUICK WORD ABOUT FIRST AID

Juliana studies some first-aid facts in preparation for her exams. Regardless of when you read this book, please don't follow them. First-aid instruction changes over the years, and what's in here may no longer be accurate by the time you read this. For example, when I did my lifeguard certification in the 1990s, we were instructed to place a leg between a standing person's legs when applying abdominal thrusts to a conscious, choking victim. When I recertified for my Bronze Medallion (the first level of lifesaving in Canada) in 2009, our instructor told us too many lifesavers had been injured that way and therefore we weren't allowed to place the leg there anymore. If the person became unconscious, we had to let them fall.

STAY IN TOUCH!

If you enjoyed this book, sign up for my monthly newsletter! I write it myself, so it's my words to you. You'll get the following:

- Sneak peeks at upcoming books
- Updates about online and in-person appearances
- Book and writing recommendations
- Recipes I love
- Contests
- And more!

Visit BetweenWorldsYA.com to sign up!

Prefer social media? All my links are listed under my bio, at the end of the book.

ACKNOWLEDGEMENTS

The deeper I get into these books, the more information and support I need to complete them.

Thank you to Georg Schmidt and the HOG Semlak (semlak.de), Anne Dreer, and the members and organizers of Donauschwaben Villages Helping Hands for their help with making Semlak come alive to me and my readers. In addition, I'd like to express thanks to my Romanian researchers, Crenguta Nicolae and Gabriela Rat, who are helping me discover the details that demonstrate just how much change the residents of villages like Semlak had to contend with.

For Juliana's storyline, trying to figure out how she transitioned from grade nine in Alberta to grade nine in Ontario was not an easy task. Special thanks go out to high school teachers Annamae Elliott and Erika Werner, and St. Mary's High School vice principal Deanna Wehrle for helping me solve the problem. Thank you, too, to Sara Marsh, a fellow grad student who shared with me stories of growing up with a father who drove trucks for his career.

And I'm always indebted to Deardra King-Leslie, my dance teacher for almost twenty years, who influenced my life in more ways than I could ever count.

This book can't logistically come together without my publishing team: Heather Wright, my writing coach and consulting editor; Susan Fish, my editor; and Michelle Fairbanks of Fresh Design, my graphic designer. Also special thanks to Kyle Bergum for helping me evaluate the first large-print editions for this series and to Ali MacGee for her advice and mentorship.

Thank you, too, to my writing family, the Professional Writers Association of Canada, whose members support my writing and give me feedback on various aspects of these projects when asked. For this story, a shout-out to Jennifer Lewington for some help with the loose-animals scene.

And last, my family: Mom & Dad, my sister's family, and Corey, Khristopher, and Jonnathan. Thank you for continuing to encourage and support me in my writing.

ABOUT LORI

Photo by Erin Watt Photography

Lori Wolf-Heffner is a former competitive dancer, dance teacher, and theatre manager. She was a member of the first Canadian National Tap Team, back in 1996, under the leadership of Bonnie Dyer, with choreographer Mathew Clark. She's written for *Dance Canada Quarterly*, *just dance!* magazine, and *The Dance Current* (all under Lori Straus).

Fluent in German, Lori lived in Germany for three years, never once realizing just how close she was to some of the villages her ancestors left to migrate to Eastern Europe in the 1700s.

Lori lives in Waterloo, Ontario, Canada, with her

husband and two sons. She is a member of The Writers' Union of Canada and the Alliance of Independent Authors.

facebook.com/loriwolfheffner

twitter.com/LoriWolfHeffner

instagram.com/loriwolfheffner

goodreads.com/lori_wolf-heffner

bookbub.com/author/lori-wolf-heffner

pinterest.com/loriwolfheffner

amazon.com/author/loriwolfheffner